Dancing In Slow Time

A novel
by Gracie Stella Cook

Back Cover photograph of tuxedo cat by Patty Bowman

Said ABOUT HORSES & MULES:

When a horse has a rough trailer ride, the horse remembers the trailer.

When a mule has a rough trailer ride, the mule remembers the trailer and who hauled it.

You can give horses commanding signals about what you want them to do.

With a mule, you need to make requests.

DANCING IN SLOW TIME

Prologue: On the Bus (February 1968)

Muriel Dunphy boarded the bus early; she wanted a window seat. In spite of finding one, and until the bus reached the highway outside of Tylertown, she looked down at the large quilted handbag in her lap. She hadn't wished to look back while leaving her hometown. She wanted to look ahead to where she was going at age sixty-seven.

With her hands holding on to the cloth material of her floral-print shoulder bag, and knowing that her ancient suitcase was stashed in the luggage hold beneath the bus, with her new carryall travel bag secured in the bus interior's overhead rack, Muriel finally turned her attention to looking outside the window beside her.

The dismal gray view of Tylertown's outlying factories and shopping malls fading away behind her, Muriel contented herself with gazing through the bus window at rural fields and pastures seeming to rush past as though they hurried in the other direction from where she went. Occasionally she was rather cheered by the sight of cows or horses grazing, and by momentary glimpses of old farm houses and barns, but the bus and its occupants remained in the flats at first.

Until they reached the vicinity of the river and mountains, she felt free to turn her mind loose in the past. In many senses freedom was new to her, even at her advanced age, and she willingly indulged in this opportunity presented to her.

A Tylertown traditional two-story house, until going on one year ago, her parents' house, had been her only home. All through high school (Muriel had not attended college), she lived there with her father and mother. She was an only child. Throughout her working life, full-time and later part-time, Muriel lived with both or one of her parents.

As a high school senior, she had learned that another student, a girl known to her, planned to leave Tylertown to journey to a city in another state and find work there. When Muriel saw this student in the school hall after classes one day, she could not resist saying something to her.

"Mary Beth," Muriel began, "I heard you were moving out of town on your own after you graduate. Is that true?"

"Yes, I am. I'm going to New York," was the response.

"Oh, I am in such awe of you," said Muriel. "I could never leave my parents. I'll never go anywhere. You are so brave, and I hope all goes well for you in New York."

"Thanks, Muriel." Mary Beth looked at her as though seeing her for the first time.

Sitting on the outbound bus, Muriel pondered her

memory, and understood that the other high school students in her class never knew her. Hardly anyone knew her. She kept many of her thoughts and feelings to herself, so almost everybody she was acquainted with assumed she was content with her life. She wasn't. She was only afraid of any other possibility.

Never popular with those her age, Muriel was more comfortable and spent most of her time with older people. Teachers, especially the more senior teachers, and her parents' few close friends found her sweet and obedient. Other students mostly avoided her; she was too serious, too quiet, too quaintly dressed, too odd, 'no fun at all.' The latter, heard more than once said behind her back but audibly, particularly inspired timidity and depression in her.

Consequently, in high school, she focused on studies and teachers and stayed away from her classmates.

Before Muriel started working, her parents were her best and almost only friends. She had stayed in touch with her senior guidance counselor, a slightly rotund and generally pleasant woman in her late fifties. Months after Muriel's graduation so many years ago, during a chance meeting at a symphony concert Muriel had attended with her parents, that same guidance counselor told Muriel about a small quaint village called Mossmead Hamlet.

Over forty years later, Muriel remembered her counselor's words. The little rural village near mountain foothills, bordered by country roads between highways, and near the edge of a river winding its way toward the not-too-distant larger town of Quayville, Mossmead Hamlet was now Muriel's destination.

She had not neglected to prepare for her new beginning, coming to her so late in life. Her father referred to a person's sixties and up as their 'slow time.' Although he passed away before her preparations commenced, he was instrumental in Muriel's new life. She had discovered in the ad section of the local newspaper her dad subscribed to, and she still received because she paid for it, an announcement regarding an available furnished room in a boarding house in Mossmead Hamlet.

Since her mother's passing had preceded her father's by almost three years, and Muriel had inherited the house, she was alone. Near the beginning of her mother's long illness, in order to help and take care of her mother, Muriel had retired from her full-time job at a factory that shipped women's clothing.

Her social security benefits and owning her house mortgage-free helped, but money was not overly plentiful, although she was the beneficiary of her father's life insurance policy and her parents had managed to put some money aside for her, partly from the nominal rent she paid them during her working life.

Muriel had never enjoyed or excelled at cooking so cooking for herself alone was a truly dismal prospect. Uninspired, she lost weight and motivation, and subsisted mainly on cold cereal, peanut-butter sandwiches and canned soup, plus a daily chocolate.

Without her parents or extra money to go anywhere or do anything, and with few friends, she sometimes felt she was only marking time in a life that had never seemed to be completely her own. Her good health and her love of reading, which inspired weekly trips to the local library, kept her going but without promise of a future worth hoping for.

Luck changed for Muriel when her parents' lawyer and a real estate agent showed up at her house one afternoon. The lawyer, a Mr. Horton, did the talking.

He opened the conversation with, "I suppose you've read in the paper, Muriel, about the interstate highway going through this part of town."

"Yes," she had answered. "I guess the articles about it make me nervous. Some of our (she continued to refer to parents no longer living) neighbors have sold their property to accommodate the highway going through."

"That is true, and highway construction plans have been stalled for over a year since your father refused to sell. Luckily for you, the fellows in charge are overly eager by now to get this done." At this point he glanced at the real estate agent, who nodded to him.

Mr. Horton continued, "Their offer for your house and property is quite generous, and Mr. Harmon here and I would like you to consider it seriously. In fact, we both advise you to accept. You'd have to move, of course, but financially, you will really do quite well."

"Very, very well," added Mr. Harmon.

After reflecting for a moment, Muriel asked, "If the sale is held up for a little while longer, might the final offer be for more money?"

Because Horton had long supposed her simple-minded, he was surprised, and impressed with Muriel.

"It very well may be higher," he said. "Substantially higher even. But we should not wait too long to accept, or they may tire of dealing with us, and think of another way around their problem." This was as honest an answer as he was prepared to give.

Muriel gave a little nod before she spoke, "Let us tell them this: You gentlemen have my every confidence; however, as much as I am inclined to accept an offer commensurate with my property's worth, I am also under great difficulty in managing to move and uproot my life. I have lived in this house all my life. I am also retired and have limited funds. As I am over 66 years old and on my own, I estimate it would take me a minimum of four-plus months to move out."

Alarmed, Mr. Harmon stammered, "But missus, their current generosity is directly related to how quickly the highway may be put through! If it would take you that long to move, they may rescind the offer!"

Casually waving his words away, Muriel countered with, "If their subsequent offer is lucrative enough, and with promise of a short escrow, I will, with your approval, Mr. Horton, sign the contract Mr. Harmon prepares. When escrow closes, I should be able to move and vacate within ten days. Will that suffice, gentlemen?"

Horton swiftly rose to his feet and offered his hand for her to shake. Although he felt like literally applauding her, instead he allowed his enthusiasm for her response into his voice.

"Miss Dunphy, that will be excellent! Be assured of an acceptable offer, and that, upon your approval of said offer and sale, your bank will notify you of deposit within the upcoming few weeks. Thank you. It has been a pleasure working with you. If you have questions or need assistance, feel free to contact my office. You have the phone number. Good day."

Mr. Harmon and Muriel also stood, and she shook hands with both of the men and walked them to the door on their way out. At a living room window, she watched as they drove away in Mr. Horton's automobile. Then she semi-collapsed into an overstuffed chair and came close to weeping with relief and exhaustion.

Over a year prior, when her father knew that his life was nearing its close, he had filled Muriel in on all details regarding the building of the highway and the need to sell the house and property.

He had thoroughly coached her.

First, he filled her in on his initial refusal to sell. He then told her about attorney Mark Horton's necessary knowledge of his kidney failure and limited time left. Her father carefully made sure she realized that the family lawyer and the real estate agent handling the transaction would assume that she would be an easy sell, as long as they did not approach her too soon.

Jim Dunphy relayed his views to his daughter, "An advantage of being underestimated, and since you are quiet, you often will be, is that you have the element of surprise on your side. No one expects you to be informed, which is pretty absurd, considering that while loudmouths are usually uninformed, listeners seldom are. As a rule, I find that much useful knowledge lies in possession of the introverted few."

Muriel's father then filled her in on some legalese-sounding vocabulary to pepper her statements with. She had used a few words normally too formal for her, to bolster her confidence.

The bus turned toward the foothills and the river, and Muriel returned her focus to the present. Although she did not show it, she was becoming excited about her move and prospects for a new adventure.

A week and a half earlier, she had called about the newspaper ad and received a phone number for a Mrs. Vinterbos, the owner of 'Mrs. V's Boarding House' in Mossmead Hamlet. Mrs. Vinterbos informed Muriel that a room was available and Muriel wired the deposit to her. Muriel was on her way to a new life.

She pulled the cord to ring for her bus stop after she heard the driver call out, "Mrs. V's Boarding House, first stop this area. Next stop is downtown Mossmead Hamlet."

After turning left and pulling over, stopping and securing the bus, the driver got off the bus and helped Muriel get her luggage situated and pointed out her path.

"Go straight for one block towards the mountains, ma'am, then turn left and walk halfway down another. It's the only big old Victorian building on Canary Lane, left side of the block."

Thanking the driver, Muriel walked forward with some anxiety, a little hope, and few expectations.

Chapter 1: Arrival at Mrs. V's

As Muriel stepped out along the sidewalk, she looked straight ahead with determination. She did not wish to arrive too late and be a bother to her landlady.

When she turned left at the corner, onto Canary Lane, she gasped in wonder, walked forward past several properties, and paused to admire from the sidewalk in front of the house next door the uniquely amazing building in the center of the block.

Painted Sapphire blue, the three-story building dazzled with decorative arches, ornate gables, canted bay windows, a tower, several turrets and what appeared to be a wraparound porch. Unable to see the extent of the broad, covered porch, Muriel moved over to the sidewalk in front of the boarding house.

Yes, she could see the porch continuing all the way across the front of the building and extending along the sides as well. Arrayed with charming groups of vintage chairs, a settee, a lengthy and fabric-festooned swing suspended on thick sturdy chains from the porch's roof, even two rocking chairs, plus two outdoor tables, with seating, arranged one on each side of the housefront, the majestic porch invited exploration.

Muriel ascended three stairs up to the porch, put her suitcase and carryall down, and took several steps forward to the imposing stout wooden front door. She used the antique iron door-knocker, a maned lion's head holding a ring in his mouth.

After giving three successive taps, she backed up two strides and waited. Moments later, the door opened and a remarkable woman, having quickly regarded Muriel's luggage, greeted her new boarder.

"You must be Miss Muriel Dunphy. Welcome, honey, and come right on in! I'm Trudy Vinterbos, the Mrs. V of Mrs. V's Boarding House."

As the owner of a rather opulent residential building in a tiny antiquated rural village, a Victorian home spectacular in design and large enough to house more than a few paying occupants, Mrs. Trudy Vinterbos was often an unexpected vision.

And a vision, she always was. Quite buxom, robust, and glamorous, with her jet-black long hair coiffed and waved, her eye and lip makeup dramatically gracing a face loaded with character, and her style of costuming herself colorfully and elaborately bohemian, Mrs. Vinterbos was nevertheless a mature lady of color.

As a description of her appearance and character, unforgettable fell exactly on the mark. Trudy was indeed someone once met, never forgotten.

In spite of being rather astounded by her new landlady's appearance, Muriel felt encouraged by her warmth, and carried her luggage energetically into the house.

"Please set those down," Mrs. Vinterbos said as she closed the front door. "I'll help you carry luggage up to your room, now that you're inside. Wouldn't have been wise, even here in northern Pennsylvania, to have some passerby see a black woman grab a suitcase from a white lady, now, would it? A passerby who doesn't know me, that is. Of course, almost everyone in this town knows me."

After speaking her piece, Trudy Vinterbos began chuckling over her own statement. Her subsequent laughter was so infectious that Muriel's abbreviated giggle joined in.

"Enough of my nonsense," Trudy concluded. "How about we carry your bags up to your room so you can settle in. Please be free to take your time getting situated. I will show you the bathroom you share with two other boarders, and you may freshen up, if you like, after your trip. When you're ready, kindly come on back downstairs and give me a shout and we'll have hot tea with biscuits while I fill you in on life here at Mrs. V's. How does that sound, Miss Muriel?"

"That sounds lovely, especially the part about hot tea."

"You and I are in agreement about that," spoken as Mrs. Vinterbos attempted to pick up Muriel's large and somewhat tattered suitcase.

"Oh no, please let me carry that, Mrs. Vinterbos. If you could take this bag," Muriel handed over the smaller carryall, "that would help me so much, thank you."

"If you're sure, but that suitcase looks heavy, and while I may be older than you in spite of my aversion to gray hair on my own head, I'm still the larger girl. I must warn you, sweetie, your room is on the third floor and there are no elevators."

"I'm sure. I'm very strong. When I was younger, I groomed and saddled and rode horses, several days a week for years," Muriel insisted as she easily hefted the large suitcase.

"Horses, you say? Well, you must not only be strong, you must be very, very brave," said Mrs. V. She carried Muriel's smaller luggage bag across the lobby-like front parlor and started up the stairs, pausing after one step to check that Muriel followed her.

"And my next warning is," Trudy said with Muriel right behind her, "that this blessed staircase is kind of a spiral, wouldn't you know. At least it's fairly wide and doesn't wind around too tightly. My late husband just had to have a Victorian, bless his heart and his money. Lift a little high and follow me, and we'll get there."

Traipsing upstairs at a good clip, the landlady's shoes made a low volume rat-a-tat-tat marching sound.

After Mrs. Vinterbos opened the first door in the hall at the top of the third-floor staircase, and reaching in to the left, pulled the chain to turn on the floor-lamp, Muriel almost gasped out loud as they entered her room. Everything she saw was antiquely lovely.

The iron standing lamp itself, the cherrywood framed queen-sized bed with plush mattress, two pillows, charming coverlet and folded quilt, plus nightstand with table lamp beside the bed, the mahogany four-drawer dresser and particularly the ironstone French Victorian washbasin and matching pitcher, with pretty purple and yellow peony flower designs and small purple towel, displayed on top of the chest of drawers.

Beside the chest of drawers was a wooden Victorian highbacked chair with woven tapestry seat and back.

In addition, Muriel welcomed the sight of a vintage wooden armoire, tall-standing with double doors and a flat top, which may prove convenient for the hat she couldn't resist bringing. All of the room's furnishings contributed to its provincial appeal.

Muriel realized her enthusiasm had to be evident to her landlady, who was silently smiling while observing the new boarder's survey of her future accommodations. Then Muriel turned toward the window, and stepping over to it, caught up her breath.

"Quite something, isn't it?" asked Trudy with a faint hitch in her voice. "Probably the best view in the house."

Staring out the window, Muriel gave her answer, "I believe I could live here all the rest of my life and never tire of looking out."

"You seem pleased, Muriel. Are you?"

"Oh, yes, Mrs. Vinterbos!   I am thrilled!" Muriel surprised herself by gushing.

"Trudy, please.   Most of my boarders have been pleased with this room, maybe not quite as charmed as you are, but very happy. And don't you know, I'm over the moon, myself. This used to be my room, when I was housekeeper for Peter Vinterbos and his first wife. I have the main bedroom now, but I will always love this room and the view from that window."

"Mrs. V's" was the tallest building on Canary Lane, and there was none other as commanding as Muriel's new third-story windowed view between the Victorian boarding house and the river.

Straight ahead, Muriel could see buildings in downtown Mossmead Hamlet, quaint cottage rooftops and a church spire, all fronting rural properties turning to small farms to her right, a four-lane highway bending away to the left, and beyond this panorama below and in front of her, sunlight glinting silver on a blue strip of river as it raced along toward, then curved beside the highway.

Two short-spanning, but very high bridges invited her attention. One, a timber trestle bridge with substantial stone end-supports, set high and flat above the street, connecting the hamlet's pedestrians with outlying buildings and businesses spotted along the two-lane through street as it curved south to the highway to Quayville. The other bridge, an old moss-speckled high-arching stone bridge, provided a way for walkers, bicyclists and maybe vehicles to cross over the ancient canal following a short distance away but alongside the river.

Muriel's gaze returned to her landlady, who showed her to the convenient bathroom next door.

Inside the bathroom Mrs. V immediately turned back around to face the door into the hall and gestured to a door latch-lock with slide bolt on the inside of the door to secure it to the adjacent inside bathroom wall.

She explained to Muriel, "You'll notice that the bathroom and your room, like all other rooms for each of my boarders, are equipped with means of ensuring privacy for those occupying the rooms. And all boarders' bedroom and bathroom windows have pull-down shades plus decorative valances to provide both protection and beauty."

Shaking her head slightly and looking directly into Muriel's eyes, Trudy Vinterbos added, "I just am not messing with keys, honey, I am not. But in my own way, I've got all six boarders covered, including you.

"I have already placed brand new bath and hand towels for you on the towel rack next to the tub. All of your towels are yellow and embroidered with your initials in mulberry or vice versa, so after you've used them, please hang them on the separate empty rack on the left side wall. Bathroom okay for you?"

Already impressed with the pedestal sink with mirrored

medicine cabinet above it, the clawfoot bathtub, supply cabinet, three towel racks on the wall plus one by the tub, even the tiled floor, plus embroidered towels in colors she loved, Muriel was nodding her approval while she gazed out a window to the left of the toilet, sink and tub. The view from this window was smaller but similar to the view from her bedroom window.

She said, "I'm very pleased with both rooms, Mrs., I mean, Trudy. Thank you."

"Good, very good," said Trudy. "Now, I should mention that bathroom windows are kept open at least a little bit, even during winter. The windows have screens to keep out bugs, so are open to let in air. I'm sure you can understand why. Whether you like the also-screened window in your room open or closed is completely up to you. I'll leave you to settle in, dear. I'll be downstairs, probably in the kitchen, so come on down when you're ready."

Five minutes after Mrs. V went downstairs, Muriel returned to her room and began unpacking and making the room her own.

In the armoire she found wire hangers for her three blouses, two skirts, a jumper, a pair of corduroy pants, her bib-overalls, bathrobe, her 'good' coat, one long dress, and her winter jacket. She placed her slippers and pair of fancy shoes on the floor of the armoire, and set her pretty wide-brimmed hat on the wardrobe's top.

Even loosely folded Muriel's two pair of jeans, her

overalls, and a light but weather-resistant jacket she prized, plus four pair of rolled-up socks all fit into the dresser's bottom drawer. One drawer up held her sweaters, and long and short sleeved shirts, plus pajamas, sleep socks, and long underwear. Into the two smaller drawers on the top row went her panties on the right and bra and camisoles on the left.

Muriel placed her high boots, short boots and walking shoes on the floor in a corner near the dresser. There was a radiator on the other side between the chest of drawers and the armoire. On top of the dresser, on the other side from the washbasin and pitcher, she lined up her hairbrush, her fragrance and lotion bottles, a plastic glass with toothpaste and toothbrush.

Leaving the three books she owned and a couple of magazines on top of her bed, Muriel stashed her carryon bag and suitcase under her bed and her cloth purse inside the armoire on top of her shoes and in back of her dressy full-length coat and long gown.

Carefully, as a final touch, Muriel positioned on top of the nightstand a framed photograph of her parents, posed when they were younger in front of their house. Then she closed the door to her room and went downstairs to find her landlady.

****

They sat in the study where Trudy placed on the desk two trays, one carried by Muriel and one she herself carried from the kitchen, each containing a cup of hot tea, a small ceramic teapot, porcelain sugar bowl and cream pitcher and a small dessert plate with six thin cookie wafers fanned out on top of it.

She told Muriel, "When boarders first arrive, I pull out all the stops, but the longer you're here and the better I get to know you, the less formal my service becomes, I'm afraid. However, no matter how long you stay, I try to never skimp on refreshments! I'm curious to see how much you like these biscuits. I think that's what they're called in England, which is where I'm told they were imported from."

Muriel tasted an oval shaped delicately orange-butter-and-cinnamon-flavored wafer.

"They are exquisite," she stated.

Mrs. V chuckled with delight. "You and I are going to get along smashingly, Muriel. Isn't it fun to be pretentious when you've got absolutely no reason to be?"

The two ladies, basically strangers to each other, giggled together like conspirative chums. Inside herself Muriel was thanking Trudy for being so easy to warm up to and relax with; a rarity in her life so far.

"Now, down to business, which is why we're having tea in the study instead of outside on the porch in this occasionally fine weather," Trudy began.

Having extended information about the house,

boarders' privileges and rules, and verifying the cost of board and what was included, for instance breakfast and supper every day and light lunch on Sundays, Mrs. V also mentioned that aiding with household chores on a regular basis would qualify for deductions in future board as something they could discuss in detail later.

Following her verbal presentation and their teatime break, Muriel's landlady accepted a cashier's check from her new boarder for six months' payment in advance.

Chapter 2: First Supper

As Muriel later experienced, six days a week, Mondays through Saturdays, Mrs. V served a full three-course supper with homecooked entrée and vegetables plus salad or soup before (cook's choice depending on entrees) and dessert after, to all boarders present in the formal dining room at 6pm. She ate with her boarders and they drank water with supper and hot tea with dessert.

On Sunday evenings at 6:30pm, Trudy provided large bowls of homemade soup with crackers in colder weather, or sizable salads, often fruit, tuna, potato or macaroni salad, or ambrosia in hot weather. Sundays' light suppers were placed on trays and picked up in the kitchen by boarders so they could eat at the corner kitchen table, at one of the table settings on the porch, in the dining room, or at small individual tables in the back parlor while watching TV, and return their trays to the kitchen counter.

Weekday and Saturday breakfasts were kept simple, alternating at cook's discretion boarders had cold cereal, oatmeal, cream of wheat, waffles or toast with coffee or hot tea plus orange, tomato, or grapefruit juice, all available promptly at 6:30am on the dining room's sideboard for them to serve themselves and eat on their own at either kitchen or dining room table.

Sunday mornings seemed special. At 7am boarders in the dining room were treated to a hearty breakfast of fried or scrambled eggs, omelets, or French toast, with country-style potatoes and sausage, ham or bacon, a generous slice of melon, and pancakes or grits, plus coffee or tea and orange juice.

After 12:30pm on Sundays Mrs. V prepared cold sandwiches for lunch, served in the kitchen on trays with small wax paper bags of potato chips plus a pickle, and iced tea or soda included. In pleasant weather she ate with the boarders out on the wraparound porch, as four seats were provided at each of two tables. When it was cold or stormy outside, Trudy set up small tables in the back parlor so they could all eat, relax and visit together.

Trudy Vinterbos cooked and prepared all the food served at her boarding house. She enjoyed cooking and was quite good at it, one of several reasons her boarding house was usually occupied at full capacity.

****

When, at twenty to six in the evening, Muriel stepped out of her room into the hall to head downstairs, she almost bumped into a middle-aged woman with wavy brown hair, accented with gray hairs here and there. Another boarder leaving her room for supper in the dining room, Muriel assumed.

A black-and-white smooth-coated tuxedo housecat was carried in the lady's arms.

"Oh, I'm sorry, please excuse me. I have to get used

to other people in the halls. I'm Muriel and I'm new here."

"Hi, I'm Nadina and this is boardinghouse cat Blinky," the lady answered, giggling. "I was cuddling him in my room and now I have to return him to Trudy's room while we have supper. He's a community cat for us, and he's friendly when he feels like it. Want to pet him before I take him downstairs?"

"I would very much like to pet him," said Muriel, reaching out to stroke the cat in Nadina's arms. "Thank you, Nadina. Have you lived here long?"

"Years and years, happiest time of my life. Blinky's lived here for going on five years. When Trudy first brought him to Mrs. V's, he was a teeny little kitten, so cute and still is." Thus saying, Nadina waited until Muriel stopped petting Blinky.

At the top of the stairs, Nadina turned to Muriel again.

"Good to meet ya, Muriel. See you in the dining room. If you save me a seat next to you, we can chat some more. Oh, so you know, sometimes I'm called Deena."

When Muriel nodded, Nadina continued, "Almost forgot, during the day, Blinky has the run of the place so always be careful when you open and close doors, and always, always close them if you found them closed. Trudy will also tell you. Us boarders get to cuddle Blinky or play with him in our rooms, but for short times only. Helps though."

"Seems like a wonderful privilege to me. We never had pets at home. I always wanted a cat, myself."

"Same here, Muriel. Only critters I ever got to call 'pet' were clients of mine," said by Nadina in a jaunty voice before she descended, Blinky in arms, to the second floor.

Muriel stood still on the third-floor landing and puzzled over her housemate's statement, moments later deciding she could not figure it out. Humans were an odd species, she believed, knowing that she belonged but not sure she wanted to.

Then, not wishing to be late for supper, Muriel forced herself to start down the stairs. She had four more boarders to meet and she dreaded that. Meeting new people daunted her, so, as she descended the stairway to the first floor, she chanted twice to herself in a whisper.

"Thank heavens for Blinky. Thank heavens for Blinky."

****

When Muriel entered the dining room, the landlady and a slightly built young white man were carrying in serving dishes of hot food on trays and setting them on the sideboard. A rather zoftig blonde woman and a large strong-looking man were seated at the rectangular cherrywood table across from each other.

"May I help?" asked Muriel.

"Appreciate your asking, Muriel, but no thanks, not this time. There's only the salad left and Reed's on his way. But please, sit right here, next to my chair," Trudy pulled out an empty chair at the table-end next to the head-of-the-table position and closer to the kitchen.

A very tall and rangy black man with close-cut graying hair walked slowly into the dining room and sat across the table from Muriel. He watched every move Mrs. V made as she picked up the large dinner plate in front of him and filled it with food at the sideboard and returned it to him.

The slight young man, referred to as Reed by Trudy, emerged from the kitchen with a tray of two huge wooden bowls of salad and two clear glass pitchers of what appeared to be French dressing. He paused by Muriel's chair, smiled at her, and placed one of the bowls and one of the bottles of dressing on the middle of the table. He put the remaining salad and dressing at the other end of the table, and the blonde lady immediately filled her salad plate and poured dressing on top. Then the man across from her did the same.

Nadina dashed into the room and quickly pulled out the chair next to Muriel. Leaning across the table, she picked up the middle-aged black man's salad plate and served him salad with dressing. Then she turned to Muriel.

"Are you wanting salad, Muriel? I'll be the server on this end of the table," Nadina said breathlessly.

"Thanks, Nadina," Muriel accepted her offer.

While Nadina filled Muriel's salad plate and her own, Trudy Vinterbos stood at the head of the table and reached for Muriel's dinner plate.

"We're having roast beef and mashed potatoes with gravy and succotash. Everything sound good to you?"

When Muriel smiled and nodded yes, Mrs. V took her plate, filled it and placed it back in front of her. Then she lightly put her hands on Muriel's shoulders and turned to the others at the table to announce.

"Everyone, this is our new boarder, Muriel. Muriel, meet Turner (the tall man across the table), Reed (who sat next to Turner), Tom (the large man across from the blonde woman), Peggy (the blonde), and I see you've met Nadina. As soon as I serve everyone, Reed will say grace and then we'll eat."

Nadina grinned at Muriel, then folded her hands in her lap and wiggled her shoulders a little, like an impatient little girl. When all plates were full of food, everyone, including Mrs. V at the head of the table, looked to Reed.

"Welcome, Muriel," was the first thing he said. Then he bowed his head, along with everyone else. Although he was soft-spoken, his annunciation was impeccable and his voice carried perfectly well.

"We humbly thank you for this generous bounty allowed to us," was the prayer he gave.

Muriel loved it that he could have been thanking God or Jesus, or another deity, or even Mrs. V.

Supper was too deliciously well-prepared for constant conversation, a relief for Muriel. Everyone at the table ate all of their supper. When she brought bread pudding to the table for dessert, Trudy explained that maple syrup was already cooked in, but she offered a "nugget" of whiskey on top to those who were game for it. Muriel, Turner, and Peggy passed on the whiskey; the rest accepted.

During dessert time Peggy spoke about an upcoming social festival planned for April, a Spring themed celebration, at her church. She said she assumed Reed and his mom, dad and sister would attend, and Reed nodded acquiescence to her. Peggy asked Tom directly if he would go to the festival; Tom said he thought he would go, depending.

"Depending on what, Tom?" asked Peggy.

"Depending on what is none of your business, Peg," answered Tom.

Muriel noticed Nadina and Reed making eye contact across the table, she giggling into her palm, he biting his lips to keep from laughing and raising both eyebrows in a comical way.

While Peggy and Tom glared at each other, as if waiting each other out, Turner ignored everyone and concentrated on cleaning up his bread pudding, and Trudy seemed fascinated by something in her tea cup.

Shaking his head, Tom sighed and spoke up, "I'll let you know either way. Okay, Peggy? But since I've got more than a month, not before middle of next week."

Today was Monday.

"Well," Peggy huffed a little, "I won't count on you, then, until when or if I hear back. As usual. Mrs. V, thank you sincerely for a lovely dinner, also as usual. And, Reed, thank you for saying grace, almost."

"You got it, Peggy," from Reed in his gentle voice. He smiled at Peggy with affection and gave the impression of overlooking any skepticism implied in the final word in Peggy's thanks for his prayer.

Peggy stood up at the table and said, "Nice to meet you, Muriel. Goodnight, everyone. I'm going to the television parlor now. Reed, do you have dishes tonight or will you join me?"

"No dishes tonight, I seem to remember that Nadina is up on Mondays and Tuesdays. I'll help clear the table though and join you in a few." Reed picked up his empty dishes and carried them into the kitchen.

As soon as Peggy had left the dining room, Nadina whispered to Muriel, "They're teachers, Reed and

Peggy. They both work at Mossmead Elementary. Peggy doesn't need to work extra here at the boarding house; her ex-husband pays alimony because he cheated on her while they were married."

Tom glanced in Nadina and Muriel's direction, rose from his chair, and snorted as he smirked to Muriel.

"You're on the third floor with Nadina, so, lucky you. You'll know the whole history of this boarding house and everyone living here by next week. That is, except for Nadina's past, but you'll hear that elsewhere, providing you go anywhere else."

While Tom abruptly pushed his chair in, turned and exited the room, Nadina called out at his retreating back, "Must have been a godawful Monday at the steel mill, Mr. Grouchy Graves!"

"Ain't no different from any other day at the mill for that man, Deena. Also, we all know it," Turner's voice was deep and gravelly and somehow languid, but Muriel almost jumped when he suddenly spoke.

Reed was clearing Peggy's dishes from the table, but he stopped, walked over and leaned against the dining room's open-door frame, looked both ways outside the room, then spoke to everyone still inside.

"Tom hates his job, hates it every day. I feel for him, he can't help it. I'd be grouchy too if I had to work at a job I hated."

"Ever done janitor work?" Turner to Reed.

"No, I haven't, Turner. And you're not grouchy like Tom is, I get it. Point taken, but he's a different person from you," Reed shrugged his shoulders.

"Point taken was 'nuff said," said Turner.

"Nothing like enjoying a household preview with your tea and dessert," chuckled Trudy Vinterbos. "Aren't you due in the back parlor, Reed?"

"On my way, Mrs. V, after I put Peggy's dishes in the kitchen." Reed ducked into the kitchen to slide the tray of dishes onto a counter, walked back through the dining room while raising a hand in an abbreviated wave to the group, and left.

"Mr. Reed Mosgrove is the son I wish I'd have had, if I could have had a son," sighed Mrs. V. "More tea, Mr. Turner?"

Turner looked inside his teacup. "I believe I could drink another cup, thankee."

"I'll pour for him, Trudy," Nadina said after she gathered her own dessert bowl and teacup, balancing the cup in the empty bowl, and accepted the empty teacup handed to her by Turner, then chirped to him, "Back in a jiffy, sir."

Within minutes, Nadina carried the steaming hot tea, cup in saucer with a fresh teabag in the cup, to Turner and placed it on the table in front of him. A sugar bowl and small cream pitcher were still on the table.

"Best to let that steep a minute or two, Mr. Stanhope," Nadina cautioned Turner, who nodded and waited.

Until she heard those instructions regarding hot tea, Muriel thought Turner was the gentleman's last name.

"Second cup for you, Muriel?" Nadina asked. "Water's hot. Trudy, another cup?"

Thanking her and handing her teacup over when Trudy did the same, Muriel returned to making headway with her bread pudding. It was delicious but filling, and she wasn't used to eating such a quantity of food, plus she was a slow eater.

As though reading Muriel's thoughts, Trudy said, "Supper is never a rush job in this house, honey, you take your time. Turner and I sit here for hours just about every evening except Sundays, don't we?"

Nodding agreement, Turner said, "And on Sundays we sit for hours someplace else."

Chapter 3: The Nighttime Find

With Nadina in the kitchen washing dishes, Muriel and Turner lingered with Trudy at the dining room table, each enjoying their second cup of hot tea.

Trudy opened a conversation by saying to Muriel, "I understand you heard about Mossmead Hamlet years ago from a high school guidance counselor. And her description for our village was that it is quaint?"

"Yes," agreed Muriel. "Quaint and charming."

"Never mind charming, more like quaint and strange, like Tom Graves, is what I think," commented Turner.

"Now, Turner, no cause to speak poorly about our housemate Tom, at least none I can think of," Trudy scolded, but in a humorous style.

"None you can *think of* maybe, but I know I heard you call him 'the laziest-ass man ever known of in these parts.' Only last week you called him that."

"Now, Turner, why on earth would I say that? And him working so hard at the factory in Quayville!" Trudy then laughed and corrected herself, "Oh, now I remember, I guess I did say that, but I shouldn't have. Seems Mr. Graves feels he works hard all day and should not lift a finger when he gets home. Oh dear, we're giving Muriel the wrong impression. Are we upsetting you, Muriel?"

"I'm fine, Trudy. That was the best supper I've had in at least five years and I'm enjoying the company. Oh, and I really like Blinky so thanks for everything."

"Every*body* like Blinky," Turner nodded along with his words. "Even if they pretends different."

Smiling, Trudy elaborated, "Never mind 'pretends'. Seems like Blinky is good for what ails us all, whatever ails each of us. Turner here claims Blinky helps relieve his arthritis. And I declare, that cat puts a stopper on my temper at times!"

Then, checking Muriel's facial expression, Mrs. V added, "Do not worry, sweetie, I am sure you will never do anything to bring out my temper. I'm betting that, even as a child, you did not do anything very troublesome. Am I right about that?"

"Yes, I have always heard about what a good girl I am," Muriel admitted with regret.

Appearing in the open doorway between kitchen and dining room while she wiped a clean salad plate with a dishtowel, Nadina spoke up.

"That's where we're different, Muriel. I'm always hearing about what a good girl I'm not!"

After joining in their laughter, Muriel became aware of how relaxed she felt, particularly with these three people, and how she had hopes of somehow belonging in this Victorian boarding house in its tiny antiquated village.

Later, but before ten o'clock, Muriel, Nadina, and Reed climbed the staircase to the third floor together. Reed said goodnight to the two ladies and walked back the hall to his room.

"Such a gent," whispered Nadina to Muriel as soon as Reed closed his door. "Tom Graves is right about one thing; we are the third-floor luckies, Muriel. For all the right reasons though. Sleep good, and I'll see you tomorrow at breakfast."

"Goodnight, Nadina," Muriel also whispered, but before she could open the door to her room, Nadina stepped close to her side, putting an arm around her shoulders.

"Almost forgot to ask. Do you need the bathroom early in the morning? Reed usually has his bath before work so he's in there before six in the morning but he is quick. He knows my schedule – I'm mostly a late afternoon bather myself. Is all that okay for you?"

"That's ideal for me. I like to have a bath at night before I go to bed. Do you need the bathroom before I go in there?"

"Yep, I have to pee. Reed always uses the community john downstairs on the first floor before he comes upstairs. He's so considerate of ladies, it kills me, Muriel! Even in this quiet town, I can't get used to gentlemen. Thanks for waiting for the bathroom. I'll knock on your door when I'm done."

"Perfect. Thanks, Nadina," Muriel replied as she entered her room. She was pondering Nadina's expression 'the community john' and smiling about it to herself.

****

After a wonderfully warm bath and dressing in her pajamas, sleep-socks, slippers and bathrobe, Muriel brushed her teeth, then returned to her room, where she put away her travel outfit and toothbrush cup.

She moved two of her books and one magazine to the top of her armoire, beside her hat. The third book she placed under her parents' framed photograph on her nightstand. Keeping one magazine in hand, Muriel turned on the lamp beside her bed and crossed the room to turn off the standing light by her closed door.

With her slippers arranged on the floor next to the nightstand, she settled on top of the bedcovers, propped the magazine on her bent-at-the-knees raised legs, and leafed through the pages, looking at the pictures. After her journey and first day, she felt too exhausted to read any of the articles and at the same time, a little too keyed up to concentrate anyway.

In a few minutes she closed the magazine and opened the single drawer in the nightstand. When she attempted to slide the magazine into the drawer, it would not fit all the way inside. Something far in the back of the drawer must be impeding the magazine.

Puzzled, Muriel left the magazine on the bed and pulled the drawer out as far as she felt she could without removing it. Although she couldn't see anything, when she pushed her hand far back in the drawer, she touched what felt like an enlarged playing card. Carefully she worked the card to the front of the drawer, and looked at it.

Decidedly larger and thicker than a card from any deck of cards Muriel had ever seen, it did have a similar rectangular shape. The card was facedown and had a solid black back except for small printed letters 'MLMeros' in white in the lower left corner.

Muriel picked up the card and turned it over so she could see the black-and-white photograph on the front of it. Never before in her life had she seen anything like this photograph. Pictured in a frontal three-quarter view from the top of his head to above his knees, a man, naked except for leather-appearing straps crisscrossing his chest. He was pleasuring himself.

Muriel dropped the picture card on the floor.

Shocked and upset, she sat upright on her bed and attempted to slow her breathing and soothe her racing thoughts. Surely, this was not something done on purpose; someone, maybe a previous boarder, had accidentally left this in the nightstand drawer. The card could not be seen even with the drawer opened more than halfway.

Peering down at the card lying face-down on the floor, Muriel found her own curiosity about the picture was disturbing her almost as much as her discovery of it.

She thought to herself, 'This is silly. It's a photograph. You cannot be threatened by a photograph.'

Muriel took her magazine off the bed and, bending down at her waist, placed it on a single open shelf built into the nightstand over halfway down its wooden legs. Then she reached over and picked up the picture card.

She sat up in bed and this time she held the card with her fingers covering the picture below the man's face and neck. Studying his face, she first noticed his handsome, but not without character, features and then concentrated on his facial expression. His lips were barely parted, nevertheless gave the impression of a faint hint of a kiss, or maybe a snarl. Or was she imagining this?

His half-lidded eyes held her attention transfixed. Deep inside those eyes, Muriel detected an unlikely combination of vulnerability and defiance. Looking closer, also persuasion. The man's demeanor drew her in, toward him.

With some trepidation, she drew her knees up and placed the back of the card against her legs while she held the picture with her fingers at its edges. Now she saw the man's body as well. His build was athletic in a natural earthy outdoor sort of way and very masculinely attractive, very sexy. The photograph was seductive.

He was seducing the beholder of his photograph, but who was taking the picture? That seductive expression was aimed at the camera. Also, at the person behind the camera?

But she could not distract herself by wondering about the photographer for long. Finding that she was fascinated by the man in the photo, by everything about him, Muriel was disconcerted by how he made her feel, and why. Especially now, at her age.

****

During her high school years, boys paid very little attention to Muriel; no one asked her out on a date. Sadly, this did not surprise her, partly since her mother had once commented about how Muriel's appearance was 'not exactly pretty or alluring so her attraction for the opposite sex would have to be how considerate and kind she was'. Muriel knew she was ridiculously shy as well.

Muriel expected boys to ignore her and they did.

When she was working full-time at the clothing factory, chances for socialization eventually changed with both genders. Over decades at the factory, Muriel made friends with two female coworkers. Remarkedly to her own mind, she got along with slightly naughtier ladies. One of Muriel's friends, Nettie was married with children, but she had a sarcastic tongue and sardonic attitude, and she and Muriel made each other laugh frequently.

Muriel also got along well with Jayne from the shipping department but did not work as closely with her. Jayne was single and a little rough and tumble but she loved to laugh and liked encouraging Muriel to let go of some of her shy reserve. Jayne had a steady boyfriend named Kurt, so she set Muriel up for a date with Ed, a mutual friend of hers and Kurt's.

Thin, blonde and sharp in appearance, Ed took Muriel dancing at a local bar and club in Tylertown. Before they danced, they sat at a table near the bar and he drank two beers and she took a few sips of one. Ed was talkative which worked well for Muriel. She was very nervous and tentative when they danced but he had patience and she improved and enjoyed their partnership on the dance floor.

However, when they left the club and crossed the parking lot to his truck, Ed made an offhand comment that upset Muriel. He used a derogatory word to describe someone of a racial minority, and Muriel's parents had taught her that kind of language was wrong and harmful. Until this point, she had found him rather attractive, but now she was afraid of him.

She had to get into his truck with him because he was her only way home this late at night; it was after 10:30

already. As soon as Muriel sat down in the truck, Ed held hands with her and drew her closer to him. He kissed her and she allowed it by freezing. When she did not respond to his kisses after he put both arms around her and became more forceful in his advances, he suddenly stopped kissing her and let her go, to her tremendous relief although she knew she was way too old to be acting like a debutante.

Ed told her, "I'd better get you home now. Next time you might want to try actually drinking your beer."

His voice sounded clipped and sarcastic but also amused in a dry way. She immediately supposed he knew there would be no 'next time' with her.

And there wasn't, she never heard from him again. But she found she didn't honestly care.

A few weeks later Jayne set Muriel up with a date with Howard, Jayne's divorced brother. This made Muriel excessively nervous because she worried that if she didn't accept, she would lose Jayne's friendship and she might also have difficulties at work because of that.

Like his older sister, "Ward" was tall with dark wavy hair and was robust and vigorous but easygoing in manner. Also, like Jayne, he wore eyeglasses but was not in the least way bookish. Although he was a little younger than she was, Muriel felt more at home with him than she had with Ed. With one exception.

Ward brought her a present, a record album, the soundtrack to the movie "Gone With The Wind." Muriel had no idea of how to respond to this. Not only was she not comfortable receiving a gift on a first date with someone, she was unsure about his choice of movie music for her. Did his choice of movies signify a similar mindset to Ed's?

And she stressed over being obligated to him, and in more ways than just a ride home. Muriel was aware that she was odd, an unusually backward middle-aged woman, socially stymied and inept. Homebound and living with her parents at an age when most people would have families of their own, even houses of their own. She did not have a driver license and she was going on her first dates at over forty years of age.

Resigned to having another failed date when Ward took her to the same bar and dance club where she went with Ed, Muriel was pleasantly surprised when they danced before ordering drinks. Ward was a stronger dancer than Ed was and Muriel let him guide her during their three fast dances and one slow one.

When she hesitated to order even one beer, Ward suggested a Coca Cola with a little Ginger Brandy in it and Muriel agreed to that. She liked the taste but felt guilty since her parents never drank alcoholic beverages. Besides that, the more she drank, the hazier and dizzier she began to feel.

"Do you think the bartender put too much Brandy in my drink?" she asked Ward. "I feel a little woozy and I haven't finished my drink. I'm sorry, Ward, I'm not used to drinking anything with alcohol in it."

"Here, don't finish, I'll go to the bar and get you a Coke without any liquor," Ward volunteered.

Grateful for her date's consideration, Muriel relaxed a bit, and after she finished her soda and Ward finished the one beer he ordered, they danced some more before he suggested leaving the club. Although she wished they could dance again, Muriel kept her disappointment to herself.

After driving off the bar's parking lot and parking his car a few blocks away in a quiet dark area, Ward took his glasses off and placed them on the dashboard before drawing Muriel to him and kissing her. He did not give up as easily as Ed had, but she could tell he was no happier with her lack of response.

A couple of days later, while having lunch in the factory cafeteria with Muriel, Jayne said to her, "My brother told me he doesn't think you liked him very much. I said to him that according to Ed, you like Howard more than him, but my brother doesn't agree. I'm sorry things didn't work out better, but it's not my fault. Ward said he even gave you a record album."

"Does he want it back?" asked Muriel.

Turned out, he didn't want the record back and didn't want to see Muriel again. Muriel's friendship with Jayne cooled after that. Although Muriel missed the fun she'd had as Jayne's friend, she did not really miss dating, but she did feel like a failed female.

Since Muriel had studied hard in high school and been a very conscientious worker at the dress factory, and never got carried away with boys or fell in love or sat around mooning over someone she had a crush on, she felt like she was a boring passionless neuter. She also did not understand how or why it seemed like so many young girls and even some mature women 'had to get married' because they became pregnant after 'getting carried away' with a boyfriend.

****

Muriel had heard about erotic art and pornography, but until this night she had never been exposed to anything remotely like this black-and-white photograph of a man she had not met or even seen before.

How could one picture make her feel uneasy but excited in a way she had previously never felt?

Turning the card facedown like she had found it, she slid it to the back of her nightstand drawer and shut the drawer.

Maybe she would never look at it again. Maybe.

Chapter 4: Only After Sunrise

Next day, on Tuesday morning, an hour after breakfast, Trudy and Muriel sat down to chat outside at one of the tables on the porch. Mrs. V began by mentioning that the laundry room, originally a scullery next to the kitchen and pantry, was a community use room, but some of her boarders paid Natalie and Florence Reynolds, housecleaning sisters and Trudy's nieces, to do their laundry. Sensing that the two teenage girls may need the money, Muriel said she would also pay rather than do her own clothes-washing.

Trudy then listed for Muriel various household kitchen chores she could perform to engender credit for future board. Upon hearing that doing breakfast dishes on Sunday mornings was a currently unclaimed chore, Muriel volunteered right away.

"Are you sure?" asked Mrs. V. "Sunday breakfast dishes take hours to wash, dry and put away. You couldn't go to church Sunday morning. I'm asking you this even though I'm hoping you meant what you said because I do attend church on Sundays and these days, the dishes have to wait until I return, and then wait some more until after lunch. Kitchen chores are off limits to my nieces."

"Yes, I am sure, Trudy. I haven't attended a church service in years and haven't any plans to attend here in Mossmead Hamlet. I really want to volunteer for Sunday breakfast dishes. Even if I get a part-time job eventually, I want to do what I can to help you out and get money off my board at the same time."

"All right then, you have no idea how much this means to me! Truthfully, I've been trying to farm Sunday morning dishes out for years with not one success. What a relief you already are, and after less than a full day here! And you will absolutely get credit against your next six-months' board. Unless you would rather have payment in cash each week?"

"No, thank you, I prefer the credit."

"Excellent. Tomorrow afternoon, I will show you the amount of credit for each week and how I keep track of it. Bless you, Muriel. I don't go to church here in Mossmead, where Peggy, Reed and Tom go, I drive my car all the way to Quayville so I can go to my church I've gone to ever since I was a wee little girl. And you know, that was a long time ago. I almost never miss a single Sunday service; it means that much to me."

"I'm glad I can help. May I ask you a question, Trudy? It's not about chores or church or Sundays."

"Sweetie, you may always ask me questions. I'd much rather my boarders ask questions than have them not ask and make assumptions," said Trudy with a nod.

"What should I do if I find something a previous boarder may have left in my room?"

"Just bring it to me, dear. However, I'm almost certain you won't find anything because I checked the room when I cleaned it, checked under the bed, opened all the drawers and such, but it was an easy job because Mr. Albright was so neat and tidy."

'Mister?' thought Muriel before she responded with, "Thank you, I will, on the off-chance I find anything."

Then she thought better of her astonishment since she had never encountered women who admitted they enjoyed photographs of naked people, but she supposed some men might like them, and even be willing to pay money for the privilege of owning such pictures. She also decided the photo was hers to keep, at least for now.

****

After their chat, Muriel and her landlady met with the nieces, Trudy's sister Vera's two youngest daughters, to set up a schedule for sweeping and dusting Muriel's room, washing her bed-clothes and doing her personal laundry (this last for extra cash), every week. Natalie, tall and slim at eighteen with a take-charge attitude, and shy younger sister, Florence, who was shorter and rounder with large beautiful brown eyes, would also polish the wooden furniture and the hardwood floors once a month as part of Muriel's board.

Working after school for their aunt Monday through Friday, Natalie and Florence also cleaned the house's common areas: parlors, dining room, study, laundry room, and bathrooms in addition to the boarders' rooms, plus laundry for all boarders who opted and paid for their service.

During her first weekdays at Mrs. V's, Muriel learned more about visitations with Blinky the cat, and took advantage of them. She also learned that although Blinky enjoyed playing and cuddling in her room, Nadina's room was his second favorite place, Trudy's room, the primary bedroom of the house, being number one.

Nadina's room was situated just above the main bedroom and consequently each room had a closeup view of a tall white oak tree, nesting and browsing place to several species of songbirds. Blinky adored sitting in the windowsills of each of those rooms, watching birds and sometimes chattering at them, his tail enthusiastically keeping time.

On Thursday late afternoon, during a Blinky visitation to Nadina's room, Muriel was invited to join Nadina and the cat for a mutual spectator sport for all three, Blinky versus birds in a tree. The handsome cat did not go so far as pouncing at the window screen, but he did a remarkably apt imitation of a feline predator in the process of bagging a bird.

Friday morning after breakfast, Muriel asked Trudy if she could volunteer to help with Blinky in some way. She offered to comb and brush him once a week and scoop cat litter every evening. This caused Muriel's landlady to lay a hand on her colorfully beaded necklace and open her eyes very wide while she stared at her boarder in amazement.

"Bless me, Muriel," exclaimed Trudy Vinterbos. "You are an extraordinary find! In five years with Blinky, the only other person to offer to clean his cat box, and even actually do it, is Carey Walsh when he comes over here to do some carpentry work for me. And that is nowhere near even once a week.

"But please tell me you do not suppose that I would be so foolish as to turn down your offer! Do you know how much time and trouble you will save me?"

Muriel laughed and answered, "I hope I will. If you would demonstrate for me how you clean Blinky's litterbox and what you do with what you take out, I could start with Saturday night."

"Darling, you are a treasure. And I am giving you a reward on Monday. I am treating you to lunch at our local diner where you can meet more Mossmead inhabitants and enjoy more homecooked delicious food. We can even walk over there, it's only three, maybe four, blocks away. That is a date, Muriel. Who knows, we may even make Monday lunches together a regular thing!"

****

By the following Monday, a week after her arrival, Muriel had not explored much of Mossmead Hamlet beyond a tiny market store about two blocks north of the boarding house and an eight-block walking excursion introducing her to much of the downtown village area.

She had glimpsed the large signage for "Before the Highway Diner" on Friday afternoon during her walk and had seen, from the sidewalk, a few cars and several trucks of various sizes parked on its open flat parking lot, but had never gone inside until Trudy held the door open for her on Monday afternoon and they proceeded to a booth next to a window. The top half of the front, side, and some of the rear portions of the large diner was covered with windows.

The time was 1:30 in the afternoon when they sat down in a booth near the back, and the inside of the diner was bustling and noisy. While they browsed their extensive menus, where 'breakfast served all day' was written, they could hear snatches of conversation from nearby booths and tables.

Muriel was ultra-sensitive to certain references so she noticed several words and phrases spoken in different men's voices from a booth behind and partly around a corner from the one she sat in, but pertaining to what sounded like the same subject.

"Colossus sees something, look at those standing-up ears…," and "Funny you should mention ears, is he looking at the towpath?" followed by "The mule sees it, too, you know."

"Hells bells, Melvin, you don't think that mule misses

anything the hoss sees, do you?" spoken in a hoarse whiskey-rich voice definitely on the deep side.

Then, one of those silences when everything in the area pretends to skip a beat or so. No clinking of glasses, no clattering of plates, no chairs scraping, or talking or coughing or clothes rustling or people walking about.

And into that silence, a single male voice, quiet but distinct …

"Brings to mind what we always say, 'If only it had been the mule.' I mean, that is the truth, isn't it?"

"Silas, you know we've been cautioned not to say that anymore in here," from the speaker who first mentioned a mule.

Silas answered, "Hal's not here today, Melvin. Did you notice? We're sitting next to his regular booth. I can say it if I want to since he's not here. Can't I?"

Ambient noise picked back up before Silas' question was answered and while Muriel and Trudy stared at each other without speaking.

Trudy whispered to Muriel, "I apologize, honey. I thought they would have left already."

A moment later, shaking her head, Trudy spoke so she could be heard anywhere in the near vicinity.

"You would think old men would have something better to do than sit in here all day, going on about happenings from more than twenty years ago."

"And you might guess old women would have something better to listen to than our private conversations," the deep gravel-voiced retort came from the booth behind Muriel and Trudy's booth.

Inwardly cringing, Muriel fought her curiosity and forced herself to refrain from turning around to look. However, Trudy slid to the outer edge of her booth seat and leaned out from the table to face in the direction of the man who last spoke.

"I was not speaking to you, Gus," said Trudy.

"And I wasn't talking to you either, Gertrude," Gus answered. "But I will say, the truth is the truth, whether it happened yesterday or twenty-three years ago. And no matter what you or old man Walsh or anybody else thinks or says, it's still the truth."

Shaking her head and causing her dangling earrings to swing back and forth, Trudy muttered, perhaps only to Muriel and herself.

"Speculation is not the truth. Not to me, and not now or ever."

As Mrs. V scooted herself back over to the middle of her side of the booth, she and Muriel heard the man named Silas speak.

"It's not worth the bother, Gus. Let's leave it. I don't want to rattle anybody's cage. Forget I said anything."

A mumbling return from Gus could not be understood by Muriel because over top of his gravelly voice, Trudy spoke to her.

"Are you ready to order?"

Nodding yes, Muriel answered, "I'm ordering breakfast. How about you?"

"Breakfast it is, so coffee for two, right?"

Trudy lifted a hand and with her fingers beckoned the waitress. An auburn-haired young lady in a white server's uniform appeared at their booth, already holding a pot of hot coffee, and simply said, "Coffees?" before she turned over their coffee cups and poured.

"You read my mind, Kay. This is my new boarder Muriel Dunphy and you're going to be seeing a lot more of her, I'm pretty sure. Muriel, Kay works the early shift here at 'Before's' and she is one busy girl."

Trudy then asked Kay, "Did I see that Help Wanted notice still in the window here?"

"Uh huh, you sure did. And we sure need the help, too, Trudy. And speaking of that, may I take your orders, ladies?"

Shortly, after Kay had served their breakfast orders

and five senior white men, those of the 'mule' conversation, left their booth and the restaurant, Trudy smiled across the table at Muriel.

"Muriel, I adore it that we both ordered large," said Trudy.

"I love breakfast food, always have," stated Muriel after relishing a forkful of eggs and country potatoes with skins on. "Thank you for this treat, it's delicious, like your suppers."

"Oh, thank you, and I know how much you love my Sunday breakfast also! It fascinates me that we have so much in common, hearty breakfast any time of day and good health at a certain age, if you will. You like taking walks, too, don't you?"

Muriel finished chewing and swallowing fruit she ordered instead of sausage before she simply said, "I do. I like to walk as often as I can."

Trudy sipped coffee and nodded while she put her cup down on the table. "I thought so. I may have another chore-for-credit you could help me with, say, every other week or so. It's one I don't ordinarily offer to others, but I sense you might enjoy it. You like to stay active, don't you, Muriel?"

"I do. I especially like to be outdoors, get some exercise, and explore Mossmead Hamlet. Is it an outdoor chore?"

"It is, but be forewarned, it involves walking a bit of a distance, over a mile roundtrip, and you'll need to carry something in both directions. Still interested?"

"Yes, I am. What is it?"

"Every Wednesday morning, I drive to our Mossmead chicken farm to pick up dozens of eggs for the boarding house. I drive my car every week, but if you wanted to walk over to the chicken farm every other Wednesday morning, that would be great for me, and I think also great for you. You said you like horses, am I right?"

Muriel answered with joy, "Yes! I love horses! Are there horses at the chicken farm?"

Smiling, Trudy said, "Not at the chicken farm, but on the way there if you walk the shortcut. Well, there's one horse, a big one, and one mule, and in good weather, they're always outside where you can walk right past them almost."

"Do they live close behind this diner? Are they both gray? I may have seen them from my window."

"They look white to me, but I'm sure you have. If you sit in the booth behind us, where Gus and gang were sitting, you can sometimes get a glimpse out the window. Depends on where they're standing as long as they're in their corral, I guess. Sometimes their owner takes them out for a walk, I believe. Anyway, are you interested in my chicken farm chore, once every other week, Muriel?"

"For sure. I'll go every week if you'd like me to."

"Thanks, but I like to go twice a month myself. I like to visit Charlotte and her family and see the chickens, too. How about starting this Wednesday, day after tomorrow? I'll explain this afternoon about everything you'll need to know and do and give you directions. Could you go early, around 8:30 in the morning?"

"I could go earlier, even before breakfast if you'd like. Farmers have early hours sometimes, don't they?" Muriel was anxious to excel at this chore.

But Trudy turned that offer down and cautioned Muriel.

"Farmers may have early hours, but you can't walk over there before sunrise. Not ever. You'll be walking part of the way on the towpath, and that may not be safe until it's light outside. Eight-thirty is early enough."

After they finished breakfast, Trudy asked Muriel if she wanted an application for part-time waitress work and they picked one up from Kay before they left the diner.

Chapter 5: On the Way to the Chicken Farm

On Wednesday morning around twenty after eight, Muriel collected from Mrs. V a large basket equipped with Easter-basket grass stuffing to hold egg cartons steady and a burlap bag fitting snuggly around the basket and its handle. Muriel wore comfortable sturdy walking shoes and bib-overalls over a long-sleeved rose-and-fawn plaid flannel shirt and under a lightweight jacket. Securely in a deep pocket of her overalls, she carried a small cloth drawstring purse with Trudy's cash money for two dozen eggs.

As Muriel walked on sidewalks toward the "Before Diner" and the Medley family chicken farm, she remembered discovering horses, in her opinion the saving grace of her life. For Muriel, the best thing about Tylertown had been the public horse stable, a riding lesson and horse boarding facility on the outskirts of town, close enough for her to take a bus and walk a half-mile there.

Originally, Constance Dunphy, Muriel's mother, had 'borrowed' the family vehicle one good-weather weekday and driven her daughter over to the stables so she could look at horses. Since kindergarten Muriel had sketched horses and collected horse toys, books and pictures. This mother and daughter excursion became a monthly expedition throughout Muriel's youth, up to and through her junior year of high school.

By her senior year, Muriel had figured out how to get to the stable by bus so the monthly visits became an independent adventure for her. She was able to watch and touch horses but she could not afford to ride them.

Slightly after Muriel's three-year anniversary of working full time at the clothing factory, she was promoted to a more responsible position and received a substantial raise. Since she had already discovered the bus route to the stable, Muriel started her decades of horseback riding by taking Saturday morning English riding lessons.

A timid rider and slow learner who appreciated her patient supportive riding instructor, Muriel stuck with her riding lessons and over years she progressed to trail riding and taking her lesson mount over small jumps in the arena. By this time, she also had more flexible work hours and could take two lessons a week plus one practice ride, either in the ring or on the trail.

With fondness Muriel remembered her three favorite school horses, all geldings. Mares proved harder to handle for Muriel, so she rarely rode them.

She always had a good ride with Baron, a stout and gorgeous chestnut Morgan with excellent gaits. He could be spooky on the trail but he had such a broad back, she could stay with him, even if slightly unseated when he bounced sideways.

A part-draft pale palomino named Mustard was crusty and cantankerous, but he had the smoothest canter, slow and easy to sit to, and Muriel loved riding him, both in the riding ring and on trails. She had to stay alert when riding him alongside other riders though because he could be grouchy with other horses.

Georgie, a small chunky Quarter Horse type blood bay with no white markings but with black mane, tail and lower legs, was Muriel's absolute favorite horse. Willing, easy to rate, smooth-gaited, and cooperative, he was a solid joy to ride and handle. He was super responsive to her hands, legs, seat, also to her voice.

Adorably personable, Georgie had quirks that turned out to be fun for Muriel. He could and would buck, but also jump like a champ. She could sit or post his trot with equal delight. He enjoyed when she groomed him and was a friendly companion but no dullard. Plus, Georgie was the cutest little horse, popular with all students. Muriel would never forget him.

As she ambled along the sidewalk in front of Before the Highway Diner, Muriel changed her focus from the past to the present. Following Trudy's directions, she turned right, stepping off of the pavement onto a dirt and grass area beside and behind the diner, and to the right of where the old canal turned toward the river.

As she proceeded past the diner and headed in the direction of the stone bridge, Muriel walked abreast of a rural property with a pasture-type fenced turnout. In the turnout she spotted a large dappled gray, mostly white, mule and a larger draft horse, possibly a Percheron, of the same color. A very tall, lanky older man with eyeglasses was cleaning their enclosure, accompanied by two dogs, one brown and black terrier type with whiskers, and one larger whitish mongrel, also with whiskers.

The dogs noticed Muriel and ran up to the fence to greet her. Since they were both wagging their tails, she stopped to say hello. The man also demonstrated interest in her. He approached the fence with rake and pitchfork in hand but with an expression of curiosity on his aging face.

Although he had handsome features, his large eyes were slightly intimidating until he smiled. His gray wavy hair was cut short, very close to his head, and he appeared to be thin but large-boned, not a small man. Muriel smiled back at him because he wore bib-overalls over his flannel shirt.

The man said, "Hello, there! You can pet them if you like; they love the attention. Their names are Ditsy and Suds. That's the big white one, Suds. I'm Hal Walsh, the 'old' Walsh guy in Mossmead. Are you new to these parts? I don't recall seeing you before."

"Hi, I'm Muriel Dunphy. I just moved into Mrs. V's Boarding House in town. Thanks, I'd love to pet Ditsy and Suds. I was admiring your horse and mule also."

She carefully reached through the wooden fence boards and patted both dogs. Hal Walsh stood close to the inside of the fence, beside where the dogs were.

"I'd invite you to come on in and say hi to our mule Leroy, and Ossie the horse, too, but you'd get your nice clean clothes and shoes dirty. Another time, though, maybe you'll want to visit us with your 'grubbies' on?"

He displayed his own outdoor-seasoned outfit to her with a sweeping arm and a laughing manner.

"That would be lovely, thank you," Muriel responded. "I can't stay longer this morning anyway, since I'm on my way to buy eggs at the chicken farm. Maybe you could help me? Mrs. Vinterbos gave me directions to walk there, but I'm not sure where the towpath is from here."

"Yes, that's the shortcut, Medley's farm backs onto the towpath. It's just over there, along the canal."

Hal pointed to the stone bridge arching over the canal within view of his property.

"See, the towpath starts down there and goes under the bridge. I could walk you to the chicken farm if you'd like company on your first trip. The dogs and I could use the exercise, and their (gesturing towards the mule and horse) leavings aren't going anywhere.

"If you'd rather go alone, just follow the towpath all the way around the curve, a little-ways on. You'll see the chickenyards and the chickens, so you can't miss it."

"Thank you, I would appreciate your company. If you're sure it's no trouble for you?" Muriel checked his face when she asked.

He answered, "No trouble at all. Here, I'll just put these implements in the wheelbarrow and push that outside this pen. The dogs know how to behave around chickens since we walk over there once or twice a month anyhow. Here's an idea! If you don't mind waiting a few minutes, we'll bring Leroy the mule along to carry the eggs."

Silent but thrilled, Muriel waited while Hal haltered, brushed and harnessed Leroy with a pack-saddle. He securely strapped Muriel's egg basket into one side of the pack and a similar one of his own in the other side.

When Hal led Leroy forward, with both dogs beside them, Muriel glanced back and saw Ossie the horse looking over the fence after them.

She asked, "Is Ossie okay, being there by himself?"

Hal told her, "He's used to it. And the more he or Leroy are left by themselves in there, the better off they'll be alone."

Muriel nodded her understanding and she and Hal, Ditsy and Suds, and Leroy the mule walked abreast together over a grassy area to the towpath.

Hal towered over Muriel but his pace was slower, maybe due to being older and having a bit of arthritis. Little Ditsy scampered and wandered ahead, but still within sight, as she investigated scents along the towpath and canal. Larger dog Suds stayed beside either Leroy or Muriel by meandering back and forth across the dirt pathway.

Even though Muriel felt slightly intimidated by the man walking beside her, she soon started to relax.

They were about to walk under the stone bridge arching over the towpath and canal, which Muriel had seen from her window, when a man walking on the bridge above them whistled and Hal halted, just in front of the bridge.

When Hal looked up, Muriel stopped slightly below the bridge, but backed up a step to be beside Hal.

The man on top of the bridge leaned his face over the side and gazed down at Hal, but not directly at Muriel.

He spoke to Hal, "We've got to go talk to young Bert Tucker. He's setting traps again. He just can't… he has to stop doing this."

Hal said, "Not sure what we can do about it… Right now, we're walking this young lady named Muriel over to the chicken farm."

"Ah, wait for me, I want to go with you and then over to the Tucker place and talk to them about this now, the sooner the better."

As he spoke, he finished crossing the bridge and turned around to approach them, across and down a short gradually inclined patch of grass to the towpath.

Making happy-doggie sounds and wagging their tails enthusiastically, both dogs immediately rushed toward him. Watching them, Muriel thought they obviously knew and adored this man. He greeted them with chuckles and pats, but gently and firmly tried to keep them from jumping up or sniffing at his loosely-fitting and soiled T-shirt, worn under an open flannel shirt.

As Hal turned to face the man, Muriel shifted her focus away from the dogs. She barely managed to keep from gasping out loud. This was the man in the photograph on the card she found in her nightstand drawer. She was secretly mortified.

Stopping a few feet in front of Hal, and a couple more from Muriel, who stood a little behind but beside Hal, the man from the bridge looked at Muriel and his expression changed somewhat; he seemed more subdued now.

Since he was having some difficulty keeping the dogs from sniffing at his shirt, he gently pushed them away and spoke to them in a voice very resonant but softer and higher than Hal's voice.

"Ditsy, Suds, quit, you two. Please quit."

Then he said to Hal and Muriel, "I'm sorry about this shirt," which called their attention to the T-shirt's appearance of being both dirt and blood smeared.

He explained, "I went out for a walk in the dark, like I do sometimes, and I found a Cottontail caught in one of Bert's old-style traps. The damn trap injured the rabbit's foot so after I got him out of the thing, I wrapped his leg in my shirt and carried him over to the veterinary clinic. His foot was bleeding and I had to wrap my shirt around it to try and stop the bleeding. I waited there until they opened, and um, they said they'd let me know how he does later so I'm going back there and check on him after I have words with Bert."

Hal said quickly, "Don't go over to Tucker's place while you're angry, Carey. You know how Bert junior is; he's not reasonable on a good day. I don't know how you're going to talk him into putting his traps away, anyway. They have to keep critters away from their vegetables somehow."

"I'm not angry, Dad, desperate maybe, but not angry" Carey responded. "You didn't see that poor rabbit. I'm going to tell Bert that you and I are going to build a deer fence or rabbit fence around his vegetable patches."

"Oh, we are, are we? And how are you going to convince the Tuckers to pay for that?"

"I'm not. We're doing it for free. I've got a few days off, so I'll pick up supplies and we can start on it tomorrow. Today, if that poor Cottontail makes it, I'm going to build him a hutch to come home to," said with a charming smile at his father and Muriel.

"*If* that works out, since he's a feral," said Hal dubiously. "Right? He's no one's pet, he's a wild rabbit."

"Yeah, true. But I don't think he'd do alright in the wild with a damaged foot. He'll be okay as a pet after I bring him home, though. Just have to be patient with him."

Carey stepped a little closer to the mule and rubbed his forehead.

"Hey, Leroy. If I had more time, I'd go back and bring Ossie along with us. I think we'd better get walking pretty soon now, though."

Carey then turned his back to Hal, Leroy and Muriel, and walked ahead on the towpath and the dogs went with him. Hal shook his head and raised an eyebrow to Muriel.

"My son," he said. "I've got a feral son."

Chapter 6: Meeting the Medleys

During their journey along the towpath, Muriel found it difficult to ignore her keen interest in Carey Walsh up ahead and instead concentrate on her surroundings. In a parallel curve the towpath followed the canal, with an unevenly spaced forest on the left side of the waterway, between the canal and the backwoods river.

Dense patches of trees clustered around both ends of the stone bridge and were grouped at intervals along edges of fields as though delineating territories of unfenced rural land. On the left side of the canal, where there was no towpath, drooping branches of weeping willow trees overhung a portion of the canal in some places, creating shaded pathways of water.

To their right, grassy meadows soaked up a brilliant sun and sent fragrant breezes, underlaid with water scents from the canal, to Muriel and her companions. Pretty yellow, white and lavender wildflower blooms, speckled here and there throughout the grass, lent further enchantment to the scene. A short distance beyond where Carey and the dogs walked, Muriel could see fences and buildings signaling farmland.

Carey stopped up ahead and let Hal, Muriel and Leroy catch up to him.

"If you want to call the dogs, I'll jog on ahead to Tucker's now, Dad," Carey said.

Hal gave a short whistle and both dogs came to him

and sat beside him. Carey smiled, nodded to Muriel and turning around, jogged along the towpath until he was well past the beginning of high substantial chicken wire fencing. Then, for a moment, he stopped and turned his face up to the sun.

In that moment Muriel held her breath, remembering to breathe again when Carey walked on.

"Almost there," Hal told Muriel. "The gated entrance is just this side of where Carey stopped. And don't worry, the gate is high and wide; Leroy and his packs fit through easily."

****

When they reached the gate with its high overhead metal sign saying 'Medley's Chicken Farm,' Muriel noticed a bell attached to the bottom of the sign, and it clanged as soon as they opened the gate.

On both sides of the entrance path were narrow fenced gardens containing flowers, plants and vegetables. To the left they could see the farmhouse and porch, to their right chickenyards, some with chickencoops, all fully and separately fenced. Straight ahead and curving to each side, they also saw a barn, and a lean-to shelter, each opening to separate yards, but also fairly close to the house.

"Hazel, get out here quick and bring some carrots! Here comes Leroy and Bitsy and Suds!" called out a farm youngster as he padded down the porch steps.

"Hi, Mr. Hal," he said as he approached. "And welcome, Miss. I'm Alphonse Medley, here to help you folks collect eggs. And if it's information you want, I'm your man."

Seconds later a younger and smaller child, a girl, emerged from the house through the screen door and out onto the porch. She carried a small metal bucket filled with carrot chunks. When she shook the bucket a little, the dogs wagged their tails and went over to her, and the mule pricked up his ears and looked her way. Hazel and Alphonse each fed Bitsy and Suds a couple of pieces of carrot, just before they fed the rest to Leroy and Hazel set the empty bucket on the porch.

"How about a tour of the chickenyards? I happen to have the time and I know everything there is to know about Medley Chicken Farm. What is your name, Miss?" Alphonse addressed Muriel with such style, she giggled in delight.

"Muriel," both Muriel and Hal answered Alphonse's question.

"Muriel's a pretty name, but it's hard to say," commented Hazel. "Hazel's a little bit easy."

"And Hazel is also a pretty name," Muriel said to her.

"Follow me to the chickenyards, one and all," Alphonse touted as they all strode on wide dirt paths over to a large fenced area, replete with chickens pecking in the grass and weeds.

"These speckled-looking, black and white feathered creatures are Barred-Rock-colored Plymouth Rock hens. Terrific egg-layers, good mothers when they have chicks to mother, and sweet dispositioned happy all-weather hardy birds. And they're cost-savers as well. You can't go wrong with these Barred Rock girls." Alphonse sounded similar to a barker at a small-town carnival.

The adjoining pasture, central on the farm and fairly close to the farmhouse, was the largest fenced area and included shade trees, high and low water troughs and other types of water dispensers, lots of grazing and a large mud hole. This luxury yard also contained a sizable flock of Barred Rock hens and two red pigs.

"Miss Muriel, those reds with the drooping ears are Duroc pigs Freddie and Flossie, our pet pigs raised with chickens and only hanging out with our most experienced veteran hens," Alphonse informed. "Them and the hens are pest control for each other but the pigs double as bodyguards."

Muriel laughed with delight and exclaimed, "Freddie and Flossie, like the Bobbsey Twins!"

"Exactly," agreed Alphonse. "Our ma must have read that nonsense."

"That 'nonsense' has sold a ton of books," Hal informed him. "Still selling, as a matter of fact."

"How come they always have to be blondes?" Hazel piped up in her squeaky voice.

"I don't know. Were the Bobbsey Twins blonde?" asked Hal.

Muriel said, "They were blonde at least sometimes, I think."

"Most white peoples is blonde," said Hazel, authoritatively.

Alphonse looked askance at his sister. "Hazel! It's wrong to say that to gray-haired white folks who might have been blondes!"

Smiling and shrugging his shoulders, Hal said, "I've never been blonde. Before this gray, I had brown hair. Muriel?"

"Um, I had red hair, but not gorgeous red like Kay at the diner. My hair was carrot red, I'm afraid," said Muriel to the group.

Hazel and Alphonse spoke over each other.

"Carrots are orange," from Hazel. And Alphonse to his little sister, "See? No blondes…"

At that instant the barn door opened and a physically fit lady, appearing to be around forty, most likely the children's mother, emerged. She carried a large basket in one hand and closed the barn door with her other well-muscled arm, both arms visible as her blouse was sleeveless. She also wore blue jeans and short work boots and her curly mid-length hair was tied back, away from her face.

"Are you carrying eggs in that basket, Charlotte?" called out Hal.

"Hal Walsh, how are you? And you must be Muriel from Mrs. V's. Trudy told me you were on your way. This is excellent, you were escorted here," Charlotte spoke as she walked slowly and with a slight sway toward them.

When she reached the group, Charlotte said to Hal, "Yes, I collected eggs just now, and if you all give me a minute, I will put them in cartons for you. Two dozen for Muriel. And just one for you today, Hal?"

"Nope.   I'll take two this time, three if you've got enough; Carey's home this week, maybe next, so I'm cooking for three, or else Carey is. Kim doesn't like to cook."

"Oh, I've got the eggs, you know our hens, Hal. Why don't you turn Leroy out to graze if you want and finish your tour of the farm," she nodded to her kids, "and I'll get the eggs boxed up for you. Then you and Muriel can join me on the porch for a minute. I don't have any lemonade, not quite warm out enough yet, but I can brew up a pot of coffee or offer you all a glass of water at least. We can have a little chat before you head back. What do you say?"

"Thanks, but just a tiny sip of water is fine for me. Old age bladder, you know," Hal said.

Muriel managed to keep from wincing, she wanted coffee. She grinned and nodded to Charlotte, who looked closely at Muriel's eyes.

"I sense Muriel would like coffee, and so would I. There is a bathroom in the house, Hal! We're not so rustic, we don't have indoor plumbing for gosh sakes! Do I need to insist to you every time? Since I do insist, coffee will be ready when the kids bring you back to the porch. And do not worry, Muriel, these are farm fresh eggs that do not have to be refrigerated right away, just washed before you use them, but once you do put them in the fridge, keep them there. Hal and Trudy know about that already. Enjoy the tour."

Charlotte carried her basket of eggs into the farmhouse. After putting the two dogs in a down-stay outside the fence, Hal led Leroy into the central pasture with hens and pigs and closed the gate. Taking off Leroy's halter and lead and draping them over his shoulder, Hal stepped back a few steps to watch results.

Immediately a hen separated from the browsing flock and scurried towards Leroy at a hilarious clip, causing Hal, Muriel and Hazel to crack up laughing and Alphonse to grin and say, "Here she comes again."

"That's Mabel," Alphonse explained to Muriel. "She in serious love with Leroy. Watch, wherever he goes, she gonna follow, cause of she got to be near him anytime and all the time she sees him."

Leroy put his head down and gently nuzzled the hen's feathers, and Mabel cocked her head to give him the eye in such a way as to make everyone laugh again. When Leroy walked slowly and carefully to a large water trough, Mabel followed along beside him.

Muriel said, "Looks like Leroy loves Mabel back. Is he always such a gentleman with her?"

Vigorously nodding, Alphonse replied, "Yeah, he is, every time too. Leroy an old soul. He wouldn't hurt nobody, that mule."

"True, Alphonse, but he's also an old mule, period." Then Hal added for Muriel's benefit, "Leroy is at least thirty-four years old now, and happily retired. And I'm over eighty. He and I are take-it-easy geriatrics."

While Muriel thought, 'Wow, you're both in great shape,' Alphonse commented, "Geriatric. Good word."

"Is our ma geri…that word, too?" asked Hazel.

"Good heavens, no!" Hal cried out. "Your ma is still young, way younger than me or Leroy! Now, promise me, you two, that you will not mention that word with my name to your ma. If she thought I connected her to the word geriatric, I'd be in real trouble."

"Could she whup you, Mr. Hal?" chuckled Alphonse.

"She could and she probably would," said Hal.

"Okay, then. We promise," Hazel stated solemnly. "Maybe."

"No maybes, young lady! I want a real promise from you," Hal teased Hazel.

And Hazel answered back, "No maybes, then," before she whispered, "Just one, maybe."

Hal laughed as Alphonse told him, "She's hopeless, Hazel is. How about I show you and Muriel the roosts and hen boxes in the barn and introduce some of the hens in the barnyard?"

"Where are the roosters today, Alphonse?" Hal asked before the barn door was opened.

"Oh yeah. Virgil in the north garden, back by the towpath, along with a fine selection of hens. They all good gardeners. You can say hi on your way home. Harpsichord, he in an outdoor pen on his own so he can't be ornery on anybody else's time," with this, Alphonse led the way into the barn while he continued talking.

"We can let the barn door open when we leave so Tuffy can get out. Tuffy's our barn dog and he's a ratter. Gets any rats the cats miss overnight; course, they don't miss very many."

"Perfect. Then we'll all join your ma for coffee on the porch," Hal answered.

"Do you and Hazel drink coffee?" Muriel asked Alphonse.

"Nah, we get hot chocolate. Our Ma will let us have coffee when we're more seasoned."

****

With Alphonse and Hazel, holding cups of hot chocolate, settled on a worn but comfy sofa on one side of the porch and the adults sitting around the table on the other side, Charlotte poured coffee for Muriel, Hal and herself.

"Coffee maker pours," Charlotte had insisted when Hal offered.

Charlotte's thermal coffee carafe sat on their table alongside a round tray with sugar and cream containers, altogether impressing Muriel with the Medley family's country hosting skills. Mrs. Medley now wore a cotton shirt over her sleeveless top.

"Tell me, Muriel," said Charlotte, "have you ever tasted farm fresh eggs before?"

"I'm thinking I have since I understand Trudy gets her eggs here and we had incredibly delicious scrambled eggs at breakfast on Sunday. And do you happen to sell eggs to the 'Before Diner' also?"

Charlotte laughed. "Yes, we do indeed. To let you know how ridiculously small this village is, my husband Clark is the morning to afternoon cook at 'Before' on Mondays, Wednesdays, Fridays and weekends. Then he comes home to do farm work till supper time."

"Such hard work!" Muriel was impressed, again.

"Farm work always is," stated Charlotte. "So is working at a diner. Trudy mentioned you were going to apply for first-shift waitressing. Is that true?"

"It is. Trudy and I are bringing my application on Friday morning when we go in for breakfast. I want to work part-time if I can, but they may not want to hire an old girl like me. I've never waited tables before either."

Raising her eyebrows and smiling, Charlotte encouraged Muriel.

"Can't say for sure but I suspect you'll have a very good chance of getting hired. Clark told me they really need somebody to help Kay out on Mondays, Fridays and Saturdays and Kay is a good trainer. Also, I would anticipate 'good words' from Clark Medley and Trudy Vinterbos if I was you. The diner's owner likes Clark's cooking an awful lot and our Mrs. V carries weight in these parts. Most everybody like to make Trudy happy."

Muriel started to thank Charlotte, but an animal-fueled commotion stopped her mid-word. Running full-tilt, three dogs streaked past the porch and headed for the fortunately-closed gate to the property. A small mostly white terrier type pooch led the pack with Ditsy right behind and Suds playing caboose.

"Rodeo time!" called out Charlotte, leaning back in her chair and laughing.

Hal shook his head and commented drily, "That energy. Where does it come from?"

"It's the 'Three Whiskers Trifecta' on a Wednesday morning!" was Alphonse's contribution. "That was Tuffy Medley in the lead, Miss Muriel. He a rough-coat Jack Russell; that's why he has whiskers, too. Just like Ditsy and Suds. This happens every time those three are together. Gets kind of unsurprising actually."

"Gets kind of stupid is what I say," from Hazel. "Minnie, Winnie and Binnie never act like this."

"No, they do," Alphonse disagreed with her. "Just not in front of the porch. They the barn cats," he told Muriel.

On the dogs' way back, Suds dropped out of the race and plopped down in front of the porch, near where Hal, Muriel and Charlotte sat. Ditsy and Tuffy continued to scamper on, making a left turn beyond the porch and picking up speed down another pathway.

"That's why I love it when you come over here, Hal," said Charlotte. "Those dogs are such life-savers, otherwise, we have to throw a ball for Tuffy all morning and keep him occupied with farm work all day. After Ditsy's through with him, he might relax for a couple of hours. Even still, he never gets tired out completely."

"We like to see Leroy, too, Mama!" said Alphonse.

"And Colossus!" Hazel added on her way across the porch to Muriel's side. Tugging at Muriel's shirt, she said proudly, "When Colossus comes here, I get to ride a horse. A big one, too."

Glancing Muriel's way, Hal said, "That's Ossie. Colossus is his full name."

Muriel smiled and nodded to both Hazel and Hal, then said to Hazel, "I bet you love that, too. I would, riding a horse is so much fun. And he's a very handsome horse, as well."

"Uh huh. Alphonse rides him, too, but I sit in front. We don't ride Leroy cause he's fully retired. What was that word, Alphonse?"

"Never mind that word, Hazel. Leroy's older than Ossie is why." Alphonse shook his head and said to Hal, "Told you. Can't trust her."

"Trust or no trust, I want you two," Charlotte addressed her children, "to take your empty cups to the kitchen, use the bathroom, one at a time, and get your study books together in the sun room up front. I'll join you in about fifteen minutes."

Then she said to Muriel and Hal, "I'll bring some water bowls out here for the dogs, and the egg cartons out here for you folks, and you can give me your money. Then, when you're ready, I'll hold Leroy while you two use the facilities, and we'll get your eggs packed up and get you set to start back.

"I'm not bossy or anything, but I doubt you want to sit here all morning while I home-school my children."

Chapter 7: A Welcome Invitation

On the way back from the chicken farm, Muriel, Hal, Leroy and the dogs moved at a slower and more leisurely pace.

"Leroy is so careful," Muriel commented to Hal. "Like he knows he is carrying precious cargo."

"He does know. We do this once or twice a month, pretty much all year except when it snows and I drive the truck. Leroy's never broken one egg. Every once in a while, Ossie makes the trip instead, and he carries the eggs, usually in colder weather. He only broke eggs one time, but it could always happen again, so most often Leroy and his perfect record are the ticket."

"What happened? Did Ossie spook at something?"

"Spooked and then some. There was a dead field rat lying next to the towpath, must have been a fresh kill since it wasn't there on the way over. When Ossie smelled that, he almost fainted. You can imagine, with the size of him, when he makes any move at all, it's a big one.

"So, it's Leroy to the chicken farm and Colossus in town. I've got an old wagon I hitch him to on Halloween and Thanksgiving, and we give the Mossmead kids a ride around village streets that never scare the big guy. Traffic and costumed ghouls don't phase Ossie, but the towpath, well, … can be another story," Hal finished in a faraway voice.

"Trudy told me the towpath might be dangerous when it's dark out..." Muriel left her question unstated, hoping to invite Hal to say more, but he did not.

For several minutes, they walked in silence with Hal leading the mule and staring straight ahead and Muriel, after a few glances in Hal's direction, taking in the sights along the canal. She was wishing they'd join up with Carey or at least see him but the towpath and surroundings were quiet and unoccupied, even as the stone bridge came into sight.

"It's really beautiful here along the canal," Muriel began. "Did there used to be boats on the canal?"

"Hmm? Oh, long, long ago. When I was a kid, cargo moved on horse-or-mule-drawn barges along this canal, all the way from up north over to the river down by Quayville. That was before the highway went through and they closed off the canal."

"And they ended the towpath then?" Muriel pushed herself to ask.

"Yeah, no use for it anymore. Most of my life, the towpath stops right near my family's property line. Well, property's mine now, except for Carey, his after I'm gone. But that's another story," sighed Hal.

Muriel nodded; she didn't want to bother him with additional unwelcome questions or comments.

As they walked under the bridge, Muriel noticed that

Hal laid his hand, holding Leroy's lead-rope, on the mule's neck. At the same time Hal turned his face away from the towpath ahead and toward the canal beside them, and did not look around until their last step, onto the grass where the path itself ended. Then he looked up and over to the turnout as Ossie trotted to the outside fence and greeted Leroy with a nicker.

Muriel had to smile when she heard Leroy's answering whinny, that strange sound of a horse neighing crossed with a donkey's bray. Leading Leroy to the tie-rail outside the turnout, Hal also smiled.

"Best of friends, these two. Been together for going on twenty-five years now. Ossie's pushing thirty these days. Except for Ditsy who's six, and Carey, Kimberly, and Yolanda the barn cat, this is an oldsters' home."

Muriel wondered who Kimberly was, Kimberly who wasn't old and didn't like to cook. Was she Hal's wife? Second wife, possibly? Carey's step-mother maybe? She was afraid to ask and not sure she wanted to know.

"There's something I want to speak with you about, Muriel," Hal said while he tied Leroy's lead rope in a safe slipknot. "But first, I want to unpack these eggs, put them on the picnic table over there," Hal pointed to in front of the turnout, "get Leroy's packsaddle off and turn him out with his buddy. Mind waiting a few minutes?"

"Of course, not," Muriel answered, stroking Leroy's

neck. "I can carry Trudy's basket of eggs to the table and come back for yours if you like."

"We'll both carry and I'll tend to Leroy right after if you'll have a seat at the table."

Muriel sat at the table with the egg baskets until Hal took the mule's harness and pack into the barn in the rear of the turnout, but when she saw Hal carrying a grooming caddy over to Leroy, she got up and joined man and mule at the tie-rail.

"Please let me help, I love grooming. I used to groom, saddle, and ride school horses at the stable near Tylertown. I did that for years and years, but I stopped since my mother needed me at home when she got Hodgkin's Disease. She and my father are gone now."

Hal's smile foretold his response. "I'm sorry about your parents, but you are on as grooming assistant, and Leroy will love this. No, wait a minute. How about I bring Ossie out here and you groom him while I finish Leroy? Ossie loves the attention, too. We don't want him to feel neglected."

"I would love to groom Ossie. Does he have his own brushes?"

"He does, and I'll bring them out with him. Carey usually walks and grooms Oss while I handle Leroy, but you saw Carey this morning, he's all occupied with that rabbit. Won't he be surprised when he comes home and finds out Ossie's got a new pal."

In fifteen minutes or so, when Hal was brushing Leroy's right side and Muriel had started brushing Ossie's left, so she and Hal stood close by each other, Hal stopped grooming for a moment and turned to her.

"This is what I wanted to talk to about. Is there any chance you'd like to visit me and these critters of mine, help with exercising horse, mule and dogs? I could fix lunch for you afterwards or we could go eat at the diner, my treat. No obligation, Muriel, just an invitation, a standing invitation if you need to think about it. It would be on days you don't work at the diner, of course."

"That is very kind of you, Hal. I would love to, maybe two days a week if that's okay, depending on if I get a job at the diner and what mornings I would have off. I wouldn't want you to cook lunch for me or pay for my lunch, I can pay for my own lunch, but I would love to help with your animals and visit with you. Thank you."

"You are very welcome. From everything Charlotte Medley said, I'm pretty sure you will be hired. Will you be walking to the chicken farm every Wednesday, unless you work that day?"

"Mrs. V asked me to go to Medley's every other Wednesday."

"If you don't mind the company, Leroy and I can join you for your trips to the chicken farm, and on the other Wednesdays, you and I can take Leroy, Ossie, Ditsy and Suds for a walk and then go to the diner for lunch.

"How does that sound to you? You're welcome any day you'd like to come over; just show up at the turnout and say hello. Or, if you'd rather, we can make plans once you have your work schedule."

"May I let you know next week, Hal?"

"Let me know whenever you're ready to," Hal answered.

After they finished grooming and returned Ossie and Leroy to their turnout, Hal carefully handed Muriel her egg basket, thanked her and waved her on her way back toward the boarding house.

As she walked Muriel wondered how much of her motivation to accept Hal's offer was due to the opportunity of being outside and around animals and how much was because she might get to see Carey Walsh again. She decided she would like to think those desires were equal and shared with her enjoyment of Hal's company. But she wasn't sure.

<u>Chapter 8: Other Conversations</u>

On Friday morning just after ten-thirty, Trudy Vinterbos introduced Muriel to Clark Medley, in charge of the cooking as well as conducting job interviews at Before the Highway Diner during the early shift, from six in the morning until two in the afternoon, cooks' hours.

Like his wife Charlotte, Clark was earthy and warm in approach and appearance, a very personable individual and easy to speak with. After Muriel handed him her application and meager list of jobs, typed in the study at Mrs. V's, she sat next to him at the counter while he looked her materials over. He was wearing his chef's apron and hat, and for some strange reason, this put Muriel more at ease than she expected to be.

Clark said to her, "You sure have job stability, Muriel. I see you stayed at the clothing factory a long time. After that, you waited on counter customers part-time at the department store's soda fountain for quite a few years also. Mind if I ask why you left? Says here it was due to 'personal reason' but my boss, the 'Before' owner is going to ask me, so what would you like me to tell him?"

"I was needed at home to help my parents prior to and after my mother passed away, and since I was sixty-two, I decided to retire early. Now that I'm on my own, I'd like to work part-time again and I love the diner. I can walk here in less than ten minutes and the food is truly wonderful."

"Thank you. That is a superb answer. Will you be okay on your feet for long periods of time?"

"I will. I feel lucky; I love walking and I'm able to stand without getting too tired or stiff. I can carry bulk and weight pretty well also."

"This is short notice, but since Trudy vouches for you, and if she can help you find a waitress uniform outfit or two today, could you start on Monday morning at 6:30 and also work Friday and Saturday mornings from 6:30 to 2:30 with a half-hour break at 10?"

Muriel looked at Trudy, who said, "We'll go back and get my car and drive over to a shop in Quayville. They have all kinds of uniforms and at reasonable prices, too. We'll do that after we eat here."

Before Muriel responded to Clark's question, a voice was heard from a side booth where the senior men of the 'mule conversation' congregated.

"Quayville – that's our Kay's own town! You have to wonder why, when she owns a whole town, she has to wait tables here at 'Before's,' don't you?"

"Yeah, Melvin, I often wonder that myself," quipped waitress Kay. To Muriel she said, "Quayville, if you see it spelled, it's 'Q-u-a-y.' If you hear it pronounced correctly, it's 'key' or 'kay,' and means a structure, like a dock, next to water, where boats come in. For a waitress, I'm a veritable fount of useless knowledge and misinformation, even if I don't own a town."

Kay's voice carried and most diner staff and customers laughed. Grinning, Clark faced Muriel and raised his eyebrows.

Muriel said, "Thank you, Clark, I would love to start Monday morning!"

"Great! Then you are hired. I'm needed back in the kitchen soon, but after you ladies are seated and give Kay your order, we'll get you the paperwork required and you can fill it out while you wait or after you eat. If you have any questions, Giselle here at the counter or fount-of-knowledge Kay can help you out. Or Destry, our diner's guy-Friday, can ask me or sous chef Antoine and bring you back the answer.

"And, so you won't worry, this afternoon I will personally drive your work documents and a copy of your social security and Tylertown library cards over to the Huntsells' in Quayville. They own the 'Before' Diner; his name is Hubert, he's also offsite manager, and his wife Ada does payroll. On Monday Kay will take you around and introduce you to everyone. All this work for you, Muriel?"

"Certainly does. I'll be here early and do my best. I understand from Charlotte that Kay is an excellent trainer," here, Muriel turned from Clark to Kay. "I thank you and apologize in advance for all the patience I'll need."

"Thanks accepted, apology not necessary," answered Kay. "Never fear, I'll have you up to speed right quick."

****

Muriel's first week at 'Before' was the hardest. Although she was given a cute checked apron embroidered with the diner's name and with two big pockets, plus server note pads to write orders on and pencils to write with, and in spite of Kay's thorough, toughly patient training and Clark's incredibly durable easygoing attitude, Muriel's nerves got the best of her quite a few times.

On Monday she had to hit the deck running since lots of folks who lived and worked in Mossmead Hamlet, and several who lived in Mossmead but worked in Quayville, breakfasted at the diner between 6:30 and 8:30 so they could get to work on time. Some truck drivers ate early also, but mainly they sat at the counter, so Giselle took care of their orders.

Friday, when bringing a trayful of plates loaded with breakfast orders past the counter, Muriel miscalculated her turn and slipped, tipping the tray. Two plates full of food slid off onto the floor, one breaking on impact and both dumping the food they carried. It could have been worse, the entire contents of the tray could have hit the deck, but Destry, who was bussing a table nearby, jolted over to hold the tray upright. Muriel could have kissed him, especially since all he said was, "Got ya and got this," before he cleaned up the mess she made.

Immediately, Kay yelled to the kitchen, "Do-over: one ham, scram-eggs, pots, and one Spanish omelet, bacon-on-side! Both have white, toasted hard Muriel can give to them now."

To Muriel, she simply said under her breath, "Happens when you try to rush for these jaspers, the customers I'm talking. Relax a little, Sis, they'll get their grub and be happy they got it when they got it."

Luckily, Kay O'Shaughnessy turned out to be a waitressing dynamo, young, energetic, confident, and superbly efficient at her job. Talkative also, she could holler orders to the kitchen, give instructions and customer info to Muriel almost nonstop, and kibbitz with everyone in hearing distance, all while waiting tables with speed and accuracy.

Somehow, in spite of Kay's star performance on the floor intimidating and awing Muriel at the same time, Kay's brash insouciance bucked Muriel up and kept her going, even though at times she felt like bolting from the diner and running back to the boarding house.

Since Muriel's break was at 10 and Kay's at 10:30 and they had to be separate, the two waitresses couldn't have an extended talk until after quitting time of 2:30. Muriel wasn't sure she wanted one but after she wolfed down her poached egg on toast and slurped up her coffee and small juice during her break so she could hurry back to work, Kay slid into the booth-for-two before Muriel could slide out.

"Want to have lunch together after work? We can take the off-side booth closest to where the canal used to be, over there behind Giselle's counter. On work days we eat for free here, a girl's got to have some perks. So, it's a date, Muriel?" Kay stage-whispered while placing her coffee cup and bagel plate on the table.

Muriel nodded yes and started to leave the booth but Kay stopped her with a hand on her arm.

"Hard to give you the need-to-know on this place and these people while it's crazy busy. Afternoons from three to five is the only substantial lull in the action. Nobody will bother us and I'll lower my voice like now so you don't need to worry. I can tell you're a worrier, Muriel and I can help. Nobody worries less than I do except maybe Leroy. You know Leroy?"

Muriel gave Kay her warmest smile. "I know Leroy."

Kay winked at her. "Figures. We'll talk."

At ten to eleven, to Muriel's astonishment, fellow boarder Nadina Bartles rushed into the diner, waved at Muriel and Kay, disappeared into the employee restroom, and emerged in a few minutes. She wore a waitress uniform and apron, and saying to Muriel, "Second shift relief, counter and floor" she joined Giselle at the counter and greeted three truckers by name while freshening up their coffee.

When Muriel asked Kay, she was told, "Yeah, she works weekends – Friday, Saturday, Sunday mornings. This place would fold without her."

After a second's thought, Kay squinted at Muriel and continued, "That's right, you not only know Leroy, you know Nadina. You live at Mrs.V's, I knew that. You and Deena, friends?"

"We are," said Muriel.

Grinning, nodding and biting her lower lip, Kay commented, "You're a bit of an education, Miss Muriel Dunphy. Surprising me – I like that."

****

Over Muriel's tomato soup with grilled cheese sandwich and coca cola, and Kay's corned beef on rye, large order of fries and ginger ale, the experienced waitress gave her fledgling the lowdown as well as hitting Muriel with questions galore.

"Starting with the more interesting regulars, if you know Leroy, you've met Hal Walsh. Is that right?"

"Yes," said Muriel, "I was on the way to the chicken farm and I saw Hal and Ditsy, Suds, Leroy and Ossie. Hal and friends walked me to the Medley's farm."

Pausing her sandwich on the way to her mouth, Kay spoke, "Did you ask or did he offer?"

"He offered and led Leroy with us to carry the egg baskets. Really nice, and his son Carey joined us at the bridge."

Kay put her sandwich back down on its plate without taking another bite. She raised an eyebrow.

"That is so different, in a certain way. Okay, Hal eats here all the time. Breakfast, early or late, or lunch usually, at least several times a week. He's kind of a sad and strange case. His wife Louise died some twenty years past; I was a little kid then, and, okay he talks to people but Hal has basically never looked at another woman since. Let alone, walk someone, anyone, to the chicken farm. But you are new in town. Any comments, Muriel?"

Muriel took a bite of grilled cheese sandwich so she could get away with only shaking her head, no comments. 'It wasn't like that,' she thought, or was it?

But Kay was not finished. "Also, you met or you saw Carey. He's Hal's only kid, by the way," then Kay smiled naughtily. "Any reacts to Carey?"

Determined to avoid looking at Kay and willing herself not to blush, Muriel answered only, "He's cute."

"Cute, he is. Maybe the cutest in the hamlet. I had a crush on him when I was a teenager, but lucky for me, too young for him and my mother told me about his past. He had affairs with two older women, one of them married at the time.

"Besides all that, he's taken. Long time, taken, then and now, and by more than one. Sorry, but better I tell you. Carey currently lives with his girlfriend Kim in the apartment he and his dad built in the top of their barn. Plus, he visits and stays with his boyfriend over in Quayville. Both relationships lasting years. Heard enough? I'd hate to see you hurt, Muriel."

"He seems so nice. When I met him that morning, he told us he saved a rabbit that got caught in a trap."

Kay said with a little heat, "Sounds just like him. He *is* nice. He's kind. He helps everybody, mainly his father, but everybody else, too. He works hard, likes animals and people. But keep your heart, Sis, because you'd be just one in a crowd. Sermon finished, let's talk about somebody else."

In spite of feeling relieved to change the subject, and nodding her agreement to Kay, Muriel was thinking about the photo of naked Carey hidden in her nightstand drawer. She wondered if she had knowledge about Carey Walsh that most people in town didn't have, and that she was not inclined to share. With anyone.

Kay continued, "Okay, the old guys' table. Always, every single day, Silas, Gus, Melvin, old Bert, and sometimes, Mac. That table is mine but in case I get lucky enough to get a vacation, you'll need to deal with them. But relax because they're just a bunch of blowhards. Play along, ignore them, sass them back, or keep your own counsel with them, you'll be fine. 'Course, if Hal Walsh is in here, it can get testy. But you'll side with Hal and Hal can handle them, so you'll be fine.

"Bottom line, Muriel, customers be damned, Clark likes you. That's number one around here. Clark likes you; Trudy likes you; I like you; Destry and Nadina like you; Giselle even likes you; and Antoine likes everybody. And big bonus, Hal Walsh likes you, so piece – of – cake. You'll be fine."

****

On the following Monday, after her shift, Muriel was joined for lunch by Trudy Vinterbos, and the conversation was completely different. Muriel was telling her landlady how much she enjoyed walking the towpath, and Trudy suddenly expounded on that subject.

"Yes, it is pretty walking there, with the flowers and trees and the canal in the sun. But I'll tell you why it makes me nervous if it's even a little bit dark out. Peter, my late husband, and I used to walk on the towpath around dusk, you know, late in spring and summer, and on into the beginning of fall when the leaves are changing colors. It was quiet and peaceful, and we both enjoyed our walks. But then, after the murder, it changed for me."

"The murder?" whispered Muriel.

"Yes, ma'am. A dead body was found just off the towpath," Trudy answered in a softened voice. "Now, this was twenty-some years ago. Peter and I were practically newlyweds, if you can imagine that. Peter still loved walking there, and I was alright with it as long as the sun was shining. But at dusk, that was not good for me. Too dark. You're going to think I'm crazy if I tell you about this, Muriel."

"No, please go ahead. I want to listen. I'd rather know what happened."

"Well, the first time we walked at dusk, after the victim was found, I got really spooked, right after we walked under the bridge on our way home. Muriel, I felt like the air changed, like I could feel something horrible happening, someone in pain. And the fear, and anger. Such a terrible rage. Then I felt like I couldn't get my breath, like I truly could not breathe! I told Peter I would never walk there in dusk or after dark again. He was disappointed, even walked there by himself, but I still refused. That's why I don't want you walking there unless the sun's up."

Muriel responded, "I understand, Trudy. I won't go near there after dark. Don't worry about me, please."

With a sigh, Trudy said, "Thank you, darling. That horror stays there, in the place near where it happened. I don't know how or why, but it does. For me, it does. I'm glad you believe me and understand. Not everyone does."

Muriel said, "I believe in haunts; I always have."

Said Trudy Vinterbos, "So do I."

****

During nearly all afterwork lunches, Muriel had company. On Mondays she ate with Trudy, on Fridays, Kay joined her, and on Saturdays, she ate with Hal Walsh before they went over to his property and took Ossie, Leroy and the dogs for a walk, either along the towpath, or around and through two pastures and one meadow in back of his barn and house.

One time, when snow was deep in the fields and Carey was working so paths weren't shoveled yet, Muriel led Ossie behind Hal and Leroy on sidewalk going north past Walsh property and beside a street turning into a snowplowed dirt and gravel road. As they were turning around to start back, Hal told Muriel that the road they were traveling led to the front of Medley's Chicken Farm and the Tucker family's vegetable farm, where he and Carey had built a fence to keep wild critters from eating veggies meant for market.

Muriel also visited the Walsh's place on many Tuesday, Wednesday and Thursday mornings. Sometimes, Carey cleaned the turnout while Hal and Muriel groomed Leroy and Ossie or took them for walks. Although Carey smiled at Muriel, he was usually quiet while he worked in the part corral, part pasture. She could not tell if he listened to stories Hal told her about life in Mossmead Hamlet or not.

On a sunny Tuesday morning Hal was raking the turnout first, then cleaning stalls inside the barn, and while Muriel brushed Leroy, Carey brushed Ossie beside them. She could not think of anything to say to Carey, and he was also quiet until they finished and took the horse and mule out back to one of the pastures.

After returning to the turnout, when Carey accepted Leroy's halter and lead rope from Muriel, he thanked her and turned to a small section of grassy ground he had fenced and gated off.

"Muriel, would you like to meet Brady and see his rabbit hutch up close?"

"Yes, please, I would, if that's okay with him."

Carey gave her a playful smile before he said, "Sure, he'll be fine, he can't get out. But after we close the gate, I'll open his hutch up so he can hop around outside it and graze in the open, and you can pet him if you like. You're quiet, you won't scare him."

The fence and gate surrounding the rabbit hutch and small grazing area was high and sturdy, with broad, close together rails. Carey and Muriel stopped in front of the gate and he turned to her before opening it to go inside the enclosure.

"Hal told me that a couple of times when he's looked over top of this fence, he's seen Brady peering out through the rails, either to see the fields and trees out back or the horse and mule in their turnout. I had to make the openings narrow so he can't get out and dogs or other predators can't get in."

"But Brady can still peek out?" asked Muriel.

"Yeah. But if I'm not going to be here all day, unless my father agrees to watch him, I keep him in his other hutch inside the apartment. A hawk could swoop down at him if he's outside and no one's around. Rabbits can be scared to death, you know."

"Oh no, I didn't know. That's awful," commented Muriel with feeling, thinking she might be somewhat of a rabbit, and feeling for Brady.

"We try to look out for him," said Carey with a sad smile as he opened the gate for her. "Go on in, and I'll shut the gate behind us."

Muriel was fascinated by the hutch; it looked like a little two-story wooden house with an attached wood-and-wire fenced-in small yard. When Carey unlatched a gate in the hutch's yard fence, Brady hopped down a ramp from the second story and out of the hutch into the grassy area where Carey and Muriel stood. He stopped in front of them and sat up.

Enchanted by the brown rabbit with long ears and misshapen foot, Muriel gasped, "Oh, he's so darling!"

Carey reached into a pocket of his coveralls and offered a thin bunch of carrot greens to Muriel.

"Here," he said, "you can feed these to him. After he's done eating, you can pet him, but you might have to follow him around a little."

Carey could tell that he did not have to caution Muriel to move slowly or be gentle. After Muriel stroked Brady's softest-ever fur, the three of them spent a silent peaceful fifteen minutes together in Brady's private pasture, with Brady grazing and Carey and Muriel watching him. When Carey opened the gate carefully for the humans to leave, he closed Brady in his outer grassy open-air area and told Muriel he would put the bunny back in his hutch later.

Muriel thanked Brady, Carey, and Hal for the visit, said goodbye to them and walked back to the boarding house. On her way she remembered Kay's warning regarding her heart, and thought to herself, 'Too late. My heart is finally alive and beating and headed for Carey Walsh, crowds be damned.'

But that courage of hers wouldn't last. On her next Thursday visit to the Walsh home, she met Kim.

Around nine-fifteen in the morning, when Carey had finished cleaning stalls in the barn, the turnout and the rabbit hutch and area, and Hal and Muriel were brushing mule and horse tails, a medium-sized woman with shortish but thick and fluffy blonde hair came down the stairs that led along the side of the barn to and from the apartment above.

Muriel's hopes and dreams fizzled and sank as she watched the person, she knew was Kim. Wearing a short-sleeved shirt and faded blue jeans, and without makeup, hair-styling or jewelry, this was a female that people, especially men, would notice.

Yes, her facial features were great, combining pretty and sexy, and her body was decidedly curvaceous. But it was mainly the way she moved that made her unlikely to be ignored. Even without trying to impress admirers, Kim's motions were carefree, devil-may-care, and a little dare-you-to-watch-me wedded to a certain relaxed brand of grace. She was at home in her physical self, and it showed.

As Kim exited the turnout and Carey untied Leroy and Ossie to take them out to pasture, Carey introduced the two ladies, saying, "Kim, this is Hal's friend Muriel Dunphy. Muriel, this is Kim Hodges."

Muriel stammered, "Good to meet you, Kim," while Kim nodded to her and spoke to Hal, "On my way to clean your house now," and kept walking.

Hal said nothing; Carey said, "Thanks, Kim."

A week later, Muriel saw and heard a different side of Kim. And Carey. While she finished currying Ossie and Hal started brushing Leroy, Kim followed Carey downstairs from their apartment and into the turnout, which Carey started cleaning. They were engaged in a heated discussion.

Kim complained, "It's just that I'm left alone here while you're off visiting Lonnie in Quayville! This happens every time you get a chunk of time off work, and also if you're working in Quayville for more than one day."

Carey argued back to her, "You could keep busy or visit friends if you wanted to. It's not like I'm demanding you sit by yourself and pout."

Kim whined, "I happen to need your company and you know that. But you leave anyway, and it's pretty heartless of you. I'm lonely and bored and you don't care."

Without looking at her, Carey answered, "You need something to do, like a job."

"I have a job – cleaning your father's house!" yelled Kim.

Carey yelled back, "Huh uh, you need to get out of the apartment and off the property! You could work if you wanted to!"

Stamping one of her feet, Kim fired back, "I am not fit for a job off the property except the job I used to have! Do you want me to do that job again?"

Carey sighed and said, "No. You could wait tables at the diner like Muriel does, and Muriel is in her sixties while you are barely over forty. Please don't stamp your feet in front of tied animals, by the way."

Smirking, Kim spoke sardonically, "I do have a job at night sometimes – same job you have, dirty pictures; I get paid for that job and I get off the property. Also, if you remember, I told you, I'm only 39 now. I lied to Ted and said I was 19 but I was only 17 when he hired me."

Carey stopped raking the turnout and slowly shook his head at Kim.

He said, "I have to get going. I do lots of full-time construction work, I help my dad, I do carpentry at the boarding house among other places, I have a right to visit friends."

"Yeah, and when you're not otherwise occupied, Lonnie sees more of you than I do. At least that's what I think," said Kim.

"Lonnie and I have known each other since grade school and you knew about Lonnie when you hooked up with me in the first place. And I live with you, not him."

"I'm jealous of Lonnie anyhow."

"My God, Kim, Lonnie is okay sharing with you! Why can't you accept sharing with him? And do we have to have this conversation in front of my father and Muriel and God and the whole neighborhood?" Carey's voice was not raised but hoarse with emotion.

Both Hal and Kim smiled at Carey's latest remark, Hal, looking down at Leroy, and Kim, facing Carey.

Kim said quietly, "I can't help it, I want more than a third of your time. I can't help it if I'm tired of sharing with Lonnie *and* your father."

"Yes, well, you wouldn't be so jealous if you got out more," Carey said with a shrug.

Kim turned around, walked across the turnout, stomped up the stairs to their apartment and slammed the door closed behind herself.

Flinching a little at the sound of the door slamming, Carey looked over at Muriel and his father.

"I am sorry. I guess we both have to blow off steam sometimes," he said to them.

Then, to his father, "I'll finish cleaning here and the stalls, but after that, I'm going down to Quayville. I'll stay tonight and tomorrow night and be back late on Sunday. I'm starting a job in Quayville on Monday morning that should last about two, three weeks, so I'll be staying there nights, and in-and-out when I can. Kim's taking care of Brady. Thanks for helping me finish that fencing over at Tucker's, Dad."

Hal nodded to his son and said to Muriel, "Want to take these guys out to the meadow?"

"Let's go," said Muriel, untying Ossie's lead rope.

Chapter 9: Across the Trestle Bridge

During her afternoon walkabout wanders on one of her free days, Muriel hiked past the diner and the empty turnout at Walsh's and crossed over the old stone bridge. As she traipsed through the woods, she thought about Hal Walsh telling her about the pet adoption place and veterinary clinic located here among the trees.

Stopping when she glimpsed a long flat-roofed building and kennel-like enclosures, Muriel decided she would not approach and bother the animals or people inside. Instead, she turned toward the ancient looking trestle bridge, spanning over a two-lane street that headed around hills and out to the highway.

She climbed the steep ramp to the short flat bridge and started cautiously across. Almost directly in front her, on the bridge's other side, just a little to the left, stood an oddly shaped two-story building. She had never seen anything remotely like this building before, except maybe from her window view at the boarding house, but she hadn't paid attention to it then.

The building looked to be cylindrical, almost like a Quonset hut, but higher, wider, and longer, and not made of metal, but of stone so dark as to appear black. Plus, it had wooden-framed windows in the top story. There was a brick walkway to and around it and a small parking lot beside it. As Muriel neared the bridge's other side, she could see a large wooden sign above the front door.

Muriel approached the front door and checked out the sign, which read 'Marchman Novelties' and this also intrigued her. When she opened the door and walked inside, jingle bells rang and the heavy door swung shut behind her. Swerving around to find the source of sound, she saw a row of bells attached to the front of a harness like a carriage horse might wear. The section of harness was nailed so it would hang loosely from a large flat board at the top of the inside of the door.

She heard footsteps of someone walking unseen somewhere in front and to the left of where she stood. But no one appeared in back of a counter standing high, solid-fronted and wide, and stretching front to back, but seeming slightly off-center in the large open shop room. A vintage brass cash register sat on the nearby end of the counter. There was a closed door in a wall several yards behind the counter, but no evidence of another person could Muriel see.

Although Muriel hesitated, she was enticed by tables and shelves, some of them wooden built-ins or constructed as standalone furniture, others enclosed in glass, plus two antique sideboards; and one iron bookcase, all filled with various kinds of treasure, into strolling around the shop and looking everywhere.

She saw wooden, porcelain, metal, and glass figurines; beaded and woven cloth purses; small picture frames of several shapes and materials; large fancy feathers appearing to bloom out of an enormous, stoneware floor vase. Several types of hats beckoned from a tall wooden coat rack next to a table holding a mirror in an elaborate standing frame. One rather plain bookshelf was covered with all kinds of toys, made with almost every conceivable material and in all colors, and shaped as animals, dolls, vehicles, buildings, geometrics and fantasy creatures, but nothing oversized.

Moving slowly, quietly, scarcely daring to breathe, Muriel wandered through the shop, scanning almost everything in sight.

Way in the back she noticed several large tables, topped with various hardware pieces, tools and supplies, which she did not approach. However, to her right a grouping of antique furniture items, most of them on the small side, caught her attention. She was especially intrigued with a tiny wicker rocking chair.

Browsing a side isle leading back to the front of the shop, Muriel found two purchases she wished to make, an old brass statuette of a fancy bridled and saddled horse, and a miniature cloisonne vase filled with lovely artificial sprigs of fabric red roses. Both of these she picked up to carry up front to the counter.

As Muriel proceeded toward the counter, she wondered how the shopkeeper avoided thefts since the atmosphere seemed so quiet and still that she felt she was completely alone with no one observing her. She had seen a brass bell in back of the cash register but forward on the counter, and hoped she would not have to ring it for service.

Placing her purchase choices on top of the counter, Muriel stood for a moment, listening. She no longer heard footsteps behind the wall, but stopped before ringing the counter bell in order to look more closely at two large framed photographs hanging centered on the wall, forward of the closed door.

One photograph was in sepia with a plain dark brown wood frame. The other, a more narrow but longer black-and-white photo had an ornate black-and-gold frame. Muriel moved closer to the counter to study the photographs themselves.

The sepia photo showed a canal barge being towed by a sturdy horse with a tall man walking alongside and another man on deck in the boat. In keeping with her past pursuit of knowledge about horses, Muriel deduced that the animal pulling the barge was more of a common saddle-horse size, rather than a heavy draft horse, therefore, Morgan being its breed most likely.

Even in sepia, the canal's shape and surroundings looked vaguely familiar to Muriel. And the top and sides of the picture showed signs of framing it, as though the photographer stood in front of the stone bridge and snapped the scene on the bridge's other side. The photo had a romantic feel.

Not so, the other picture. In stark black and white, the longer photograph was a dramatic closeup of a woman's face. Her face was arresting rather than pretty. She had long, very dark wavy unkempt hair, wind-driven and with long bangs swept to the sides of her face. Her very pronounced cheekbones and thin cheeks made her face appear diamond shaped, with a centered European-type nose. Her mouth stretched far across her face in a grim line, her lips darker than her skin, although not at all lush.

But it was her eyes, under dramatically dark angled eyebrows, that drew the onlooker's focus. Large, black, terribly fierce eyes glared out from the picture and challenged the beholder to look closer. Muriel felt she detected a wild and wicked glee from under the woman's long and dark eyelashes. Yet somehow the fury in those creature eyes could appear hot from one angle, blistering cold from another.

This was a remarkable, unforgettable face, and Muriel had difficulty taking her gaze away from it. While she stared at the picture, Muriel heard the sound of movement from in front of her to her right. Turning her head, she saw a robust bear of a man standing in front of a chair placed near a corner in that section of wall.

He walked slowly to the counter across from where Muriel stood and said, "Would you like me to wrap those for you?"

Nodding yes, she answered, "Yes, thank you. But first, may I ask about the photographs?"

"Ask away," said he, with his warm brown eyes focused directly at her face. His voice was very pleasing to Muriel. Deep but soft, and his enunciation outstanding.

"They are such intriguing photos. Are they by the same photographer?"

"No, actually, they're not. The canal photo is ancient, given to me by a fellow who lives in Mossmead; his grandfather took the picture. The other one, I took when I was sixteen years old. Glad you like them. I've kept them here for decades but not many people comment on them."

While he spoke, he reached under the counter, then placed a sheet of floral-print wrapping paper on the countertop. Muriel observed as he expertly wrapped the artificial roses and set them aside. This accomplished, he produced another sheet of the same type and print and wrapped the little vase.

When another, larger sheet of paper in a playful kitten print was laid upon the counter and used to wrap the brass horse, Muriel could no longer contain her delight.

"Oh, thank you! Your wrapping paper is so fine and wonderful, and I'm amazed by your shop. I hope you don't mind my asking. Are you Mr. Marchman?"

"No, I'm Charlie. Are you visiting Mossmead Hamlet?"

Muriel smiled, "I'm new to Mossmead. I recently moved into Mrs. V's Boarding House. I'm completely charmed by the whole area."

To her vast surprise, Charlie said, "You must be

Muriel. Good to meet you. Nadina's told me what a lovely friend you are to her. Please accept the vase and flowers as a welcoming gift, from Nadina and Marchman Novelty."

"Nadina is very kind to me. Oh, are you her gentleman caller? She's told me how fond of you she is and how well you treat her, too. She so looks forward to the Wednesday night dinners you treat her to at Riverbank Café or at Darnell's in Quayville. She said they're both right beside the river. I thank you, but I feel guilty accepting such a generous gift. And would the owner be upset with you for undercharging me?"

Charlie told her, "I am the current owner, Charlie L. Miller, and I insist you accept the gift. Deena would be cross with me if I didn't. I will charge you for the horse, though, and novelties don't come cheap. That's why I changed the name of this shop; it used to be called Marchman's Goods & Sundries and the previous owner lost money on it."

"I've never seen a building like this one, or stone so dark. It seems highly unusual and fascinating," was Muriel's comment.

"It's quarry rock. The builder stacked and cemented the rocks around an open-ended wooden structure, which is why you only see exposed stone walls in the front and back. I've lived here since I was a child. The place has been modified a bit and added to over the years."

"Thank you, Charlie, for telling me about your shop and home. You are easy to talk with. I'm glad you and Nadina found each other. That seems like lucky happiness to me."

"Lucky happiness," mused Charlie. "Now, there's a dream to aim for. Would you like a burlap bag to carry these in?"

Muriel opened her large cloth purse and explained, "No, thank you, I have this big bag to carry my treasures in."

She had deliberately left her handbag almost empty and stashed her money in a small cloth purse tucked inside a front pocket of her blue jeans.

"Perfect," said Charlie. "Here, let me pack these for you."

Carefully sliding her packages to her side of the counter, Charlie turned around to walk back to the far end of the counter in order to come around to where Muriel stood. Muriel, already aware of his ruddy handsome face, black hair, eyebrows, moustache and beard, now saw that Charlie's long hair was pulled back in a short ponytail with wavy ends.

As he approached, she glanced quickly at the photographic portrait and then away, back to Charlie's face. Not exactly, but something …

While Muriel held her cloth bag open wide, Charlie

skillfully placed her packages inside in such a way that they would not obstruct each other or her movement. This accomplished, he offered to hold her bag and told her the price of the brass horse.

Handing over the cloth straps to her large bag, Muriel dug her small purse out of a jeans pocket and put the exact amount of money on top of the counter in accordance with a nod of his head in that direction. He gave her bag back to her, picked up the money, walked around the counter, rang up the sale and handed her a receipt. Then, from behind the counter, Charlie performed a slight bow from his waist in her direction.

"Lovely to meet you, Muriel. Welcome to Marchman Novelty Shop and please feel free to come in any time we're open. Say hi to Nadina for me and maybe I'll see you in front of Mrs. V's some Wednesday evening, if you'd care to come out to my car with Deena. Thanks for your business," he concluded.

Muriel said, "My pleasure, and thank you for your gift and courtesy. Deena will hear all about my visit and I must warn you that you may see me again and again while I look for more treasures. Good day, Charlie."

She smiled at him, he nodded to her, and she left the shop.

As the door swung shut behind Muriel, Charlie murmured, "Same." Then he walked past the pictures, through the door beside them, and into a large storage room where he found duplicates of the horse, vase and cloth roses Muriel had purchased. These he brought back into the shop and placed them in a different area than Muriel had chosen them from. In a moment though, he changed his mind. She was curious and observant, he thought; she might notice the next time she came in and be disappointed. He went to the trouble of exchanging the duplicates for a small painted iron bulldog figure and a fringe-shaded table lamp.

Muriel paused outside and read shop hours, printed below 'Marchman Novelties' on the sign. Open every day from 10:30 in the morning, Marchman's closed early on Wednesdays and Sundays at 4:30, but stayed open until 6:30 during the rest of the week.

As she moved slowly back across the bridge and mentally compared Charlie's dark and earthy features to the striking face of the wild-eyed woman in the photo Charlie took at sixteen, Muriel's thoughts were interrupted by the flash of another photograph. Another in black and white, the picture card hidden in her nightstand drawer.

Muriel suddenly heard in memory Kim Hodges' voice saying, '…same job as you have, dirty pictures…' to Carey.

While she held onto the rail and eased down the ramp from the bridge, Muriel noticed that if she immediately turned right, she could walk on sidewalk along the street and cross in front of the diner on her way home.

She turned right, but stopped after her turn and gazed back and across the street at the mysterious building she had just visited. A question flooded her mind.

Was Charlie Miller the photographer who took the erotic picture of Carey Walsh? And who was the woman in the picture hanging in his shop?

Chapter 10: A Strange Gift of Discovery

Early on a Monday morning in March, in accordance with her new habit, Muriel had arrived at the diner at ten after six and was having a cup of coffee from a pot she made before starting work at six-thirty. She wore her waitress uniform and apron and drank her coffee while sitting in the booth-for-two where she lunched with Kay on Friday afternoons. Clark and Antoine were already at work in the kitchen.

Twelve minutes later Kay and Giselle entered the diner, one in front of the other, and hung up their coats while Muriel took her empty coffee cup back to the kitchen and rinsed and placed it on a counter to be washed later by Destry. Giselle was making a second pot of coffee when Muriel came past the counter, and Kay was unlocking the front door and placing the 'Open' sign in the window. Seconds later, Hal Walsh came into the diner, causing both waitresses out on the floor to stare at him.

"A little early, are you?" Kay addressed him.

"Having breakfast early. Kay, Muriel, may I ask a favor of you both?" Hal responded. "Could Muriel wait on me this morning, even though I'm going to sit in Kay's territory? Would either of you mind?"

Kay looked to Muriel and Muriel to Kay. Kay's expression said, 'Well, how about that!' and Muriel might as well have said out loud, 'What's going on? I don't understand.'

Lifting her chin and boldly smirking to Hal, Kay said, "No problem for me, Mr. Walsh, but is she getting a bigger tip than I would?"

Hal did not answer, he looked past Kay to Muriel. His face silently imploring her allowance and conveying his hope.

"As long as Kay doesn't mind, I'd be happy to wait on you," said Muriel, a trifle tentatively. "But I certainly hope that does not guarantee me a tip of any size."

"Have at it," Kay stated, smiling at Muriel. "Less work for me, so be my guest. Just joking about the tip."

Muriel picked up a menu and walked over to Hal.

"Where would you like to sit?" she asked, knowing it would not be in his usual lunch booth located in her territory these days.

"My thanks to you both," said Hal. Touching Muriel lightly on one arm, he led the way to a booth-for-two that was tucked into a back corner and next to the 'old-guys' large booth beside and before it.

When Hal sat down and Muriel laid a menu in front of him, she noticed that the large window beside this little booth had a fairly closeup view of one end of the turnout and one side of the barn on Walsh's property.

Saying to Hal, "I'll bring your coffee," Muriel went back behind the counter, all the while thinking how relieved she was that the crew of 'oldster' fellows would never come in this early. Once before, when fortunately, Kay was waiting on both booths in this area and Hal by himself but also Silas with his companions sat in these side-by-side booths, Silas and Gus, especially, had pestered Hal. And in return, Hal had argued back at them, his voice raised, his words vehement. Even from a distance this had given Muriel pause.

Hal alone, she thought she could handle.

Returning to Hal's booth to fill his mug with coffee, Muriel took his breakfast order and put it in place for the cooks. When she returned to his booth and served to him with a smile, she saw that the overhead light covering the turnout area was on since the sun had not yet come up. She also saw that Carey was cleaning the empty turnout and he was wearing a snug T-shirt.

Muriel paused, watching Carey. Hal said, "He's cleaning early since he's working in Quayville today. Leroy and Ossie are in the barn eating breakfast, so I thought I'd do the same in the diner."

Embarrassed and a little confused, Muriel could feel Hal observing her even as he began eating breakfast. In spite of that, she was reluctant to take her eyes off Carey. She heard herself automatically asking Hal if he wanted anything else.

Hal answered, "No, I'm fine. And don't worry, I won't do this again and make a scene with you and Kay. But

Carey will be up and out early for at least three or four weeks, as long as his current construction job lasts."

Immediately, Muriel's focus shifted to Hal's face. Was he doing what she suspected? Did he make her aware of this booth in this position and with this view on purpose? Hal met her gaze with the most innocuous of expressions. A moment after, he went back to eating breakfast, his full attention seemingly on the food in front of him.

As Muriel returned to her station of tables and booths, to wait on other early customers, her thoughts were secretly whirring. Could her friend Hal Walsh possibly be this ignorant of her feelings and what he was doing to her? Or was he actually this disingenuous? And to what purpose?

Even though Muriel had to clear her head to do her best at her job, she formed a plan to avail herself of the pleasure of viewing Carey in the early mornings while she drank her pre-work cup of coffee. In the booth Carey's father had just made her aware of. Let Hal be deviously successful at whatever his scheme was, Muriel would not deprive herself of this opportunity.

And at first, she didn't.

Friday morning, Muriel's next workday at the diner, saw her seated with coffee in the booth with a view, at least twenty minutes earlier than she had waited on Hal though. The turnout was empty but suddenly a light came on in the apartment above the barn, and Muriel saw Carey walk across a small room. He wore only a T-shirt and briefs before he retrieved a pair of jeans from a hook in the wall and hurriedly put them on. As he left the room, he turned the light out in the room. A moment later Carey appeared in the turnout area and began using rake and pitchfork.

The following morning, a Saturday, was different. When Muriel sat down with her coffee in the little viewing booth, the turnout was not lighted. Realizing that Carey was probably not working in Quayville on weekends, Muriel almost turned her gaze from the window, but then she noticed a light on in the apartment above the barn.

In spite of feeling guilty for watching, Muriel did not turn away when she glimpsed Carey wearing only briefs and standing behind the foot of a bed while Kim in a short slinky nightgown approached him. Carey faced Kim and they began kissing, with Kim running her hands all over Carey and Carey keeping one hand steadily on her back, pressing her close.

Muriel looked quickly away, deciding this was her final coffee break in this particular booth. And wondering if she would ever understand Hal Walsh.

Chapter 11: Private Moments, Witnessed or Shared

On the first Monday in April, April Fool's Day, Muriel broke her resolve and once more drank her pre-work cup of coffee in the small booth with the big view. What she saw on this morning added to her guilt for a separate reason and made her sad and perplexed in a lasting manner. She would not understand what she witnessed; yet she could not forget it and was haunted by it.

This time, Muriel noticed that Leroy and Ossie were already outside in their lighted turnout area. Leroy, grazing closer to the outside fence, moved slowly out of view in the direction of the towpath and bridge. But Ossie stood solidly in place near the center of the Walsh paddock. Without the mule in front of him, Muriel could see that the big horse's head was lifted; he was not browsing the grassy area or the torn apart flakes of hay on the ground in front of him, although he was chewing on strands of hay held in his mouth.

In less than a second, Muriel perceived why the big horse kept his head up. Carey Walsh, wearing T-shirt and jeans, stood against the Percheron, next to his shoulder. Carey's arms encircled Ossie's neck and he appeared to be hugging the giant horse. To Muriel's dismay, Carey's shoulders were moving and his face was pressed against Ossie's neck. She realized Carey was crying.

Terrified over what might be wrong to upset Carey so, but also ashamed that she had continued to spy on the first man to intrigue her in this way, violating his privacy, Muriel took her coffee over to the booth on the diner's other side, where she could not see Walsh property. She wanted to ask Hal about why Carey was upset but knew she wouldn't. She would hold this secret sorrow inside and not tell anyone.

****

At the boarding house on Thursday night, the fourth of April, Muriel went to bed early due to her alarm clock set early for work on Friday. But she awoke without apparent cause after only an hour or so of sleep. Her room was quiet and dark but an unusual feeling of unrest would not allow her to go back to sleep.

Not knowing why, Muriel got out of bed, stepped into her slippers and pulled her robe on over her pajamas, then she moved cautiously out into the hall near the third-floor landing.

She sat down on a top stair and listened, believing that somewhere, someone in the house was speaking in an emotional way. Muriel crept downstairs, unsure if she should proceed and stopping in the middle of the stairs from the second to first floor. But now, she could hear voices for sure, coming from the back parlor.

When Muriel entered the room, she saw that Turner and Trudy sat beside each other on the couch. Turner was crying; Trudy had tears in her voice while she held his hand and tried to comfort him.

"He was the best of us, all of us. Who will protect and defend us now?" With the back of his hand, Turner wiped tears from his face as he spoke.

Since he faced Trudy and therefore the entrance to the parlor, he saw Muriel approaching and he flinched, thus alerting Trudy to her presence.

Trudy said to Muriel, "We just heard on TV that Martin Luther King was assassinated today. These are sad times, Muriel. Tragic times for this whole country."

"Oh, I'm so sorry," began Muriel, her eyes beginning to tear up also. "Maybe I'm intruding?"

"No, of course not," Trudy said. "You're welcome to stay. This affects you, too. It affects everybody. When will people ever learn that shooting someone is not the answer to settling differences? It just makes me so sad. Especially killing someone like him, like Reverend King."

Watching Muriel sink into a chair opposite the sofa, Turner said, "Makes me mad is what it does. Mad and hopeless."

Muriel nodded her agreement to Turner and began to cry. She had no words but felt like she could not stand up or leave. She saw Trudy shaking her head.

Trudy said, "Makes sense to be angry, but you must not be hopeless. Much as ever, we've got to follow what he taught us. We have to keep our hopes up, swallow our rage, and stand together, no matter what. In the meantime, though, I hope justice is served on the miserable S.O.B. that shot him."

"Won't be. Not if he's white," moaned Turner. "If he'd be black, he'd already be in jail by now, mother."

Muriel had heard Turner refer to Trudy as 'mother' before. She and Nadina had agreed that it was a term of affection, like a husband and wife calling each other papa and mama. They both felt there was more to Hunter and Trudy's relationship than boarder and landlady.

Muriel nodded regretfully in accordance with what he had just said about justice and race.

Trudy, however, gently shook her head and told Turner, "Now, that may not be true. For all we know there were witnesses and the sniper is white, but the authorities are hunting him."

"Are they? How hard? Look what happened to me those twenty years ago! I spent a day in jail just because I'm black and I have big hands! You remember that, right? Hal Walsh has big hands, too, but he's white and his white wife was his alibi so don't bother Mr. Walsh. And that Marchman, him and his big hands the obvious choice but hey – he's white and we can't find him anyway, so … even though he cleans our police station, let's just arrest this worthless n…"

Hunter bit his lips and moved back away from Trudy.

Trudy's eyes flashed but she did not raise her voice, "Good you stopped because I do not want to hear that word from you or anybody else. Not in my house, my home, your home and Muriel's, too. Yes, that was wrong what happened to you, Turner. Very wrong, and I am sorry. But everyone in this town, white or otherwise, is not as ignorant as that cracker deputy who did that to you. And the sheriff told him he was wrong to haul you in, wrong to question you, wrong all the way around. He almost lost his job because of what he did."

Trudy's last sentence made Turner wince and elicited a tirade from him in a desperate voice, only slightly short of an anguished howl.

"But I did lose my work cause of that mess! A course I was done as janitor at the police department that very night. And Darnell's let me go, all because of something I did not do and a white man accusing me of what I did not do! If not for you and Mr. Vinterbos and Charlie Miller, I'd of lost my other job, my janitor job at the school, too! Hell, if not for Charlie, I might have been charged and maybe even convicted and done – put in prison for killing a woman I had nothing to do with and didn't even know!"

Muriel knew her horror at what Turner said must show on her face since he looked to her when he continued.

"That damn deputy figured since I knew what she was – a prostitute – like everybody knew, that I would have been with her or tried to be with her and then strangled her to death. Why would I do that? Why would a black man with no money to spare for anything, living with and helping his mama, pay for sex with a white hooker? Also, for that matter, hang out and drink in Ted Dubbock's tavern, with all the white men that went there. Why would I do that? I never would. I never did."

Seeing her tears, Trudy offered Muriel tissues from the box of Kleenex that had been resting beside her on the couch. Then she put the box back between Turner and herself and moved forward to stand up.

"I will go to the kitchen and make hot tea for us," Trudy said. "Doesn't look like we're sleeping any time soon."

"I can do it, Trudy," volunteered Muriel. "Please, let me. Don't get up; I know where everything is now."

"Thank you, darling, that would be great," Trudy sat back and picked up Turner's hand again.

****

"Put your hand on my neck."

He had to lean down and forward in the dark to hear her throaty whisper. He hesitated fulfilling her request, but kept up with his motions against and inside her, slowing a little lest he be too soon for her. But he could tell she was close.

She moaned and grabbed one of his wrists. "My

throat, gently squeeze. I need you to do it now," she gasped.

Panting, he did as she asked, with just enough control to remain gentle. They were both rocking and making sounds, and too late, he heard the heavy footsteps behind him.

A force, stronger than he had ever felt before, grabbed the back of his neck and his hair and pulled him off of her. While he frantically tried to pull up his jeans, the monster wrenched his shoulder, turning him, and punching its huge fist into his left eye. Then, again, that iron fist slammed into him, his jaw this time. He nearly blacked out right away.

Pain and fear were shooting through his head and face when he was winded by a powerful body blow and thrown to the ground. He struggled to get up but he could not even rise to his knees. He could barely see.

Even still, even in the dark, he could feel the monster turn toward her.

While he struggled on the ground, he'd hoped she would stand up and run, get away somehow. But she did not move, not even to push her dress back down; she stayed still on the ground. Although there were trees all around, because they were in a clearing with a partial moon shining down, he could see her face turned up to the monster. Her eyes would be challenging, he supposed that since he knew her.

Her mammoth husband dropped to his knees over her, sat down on her and grasped her throat with one gigantic hand, starting to strangle her.

Somehow in his desperation, he struggled to his feet and hit the behemoth's back with his fists. Turning away from her and rising, the furious giant grabbed his throat and kneed his groin so hard he yelped. He fell down and the monster kicked up and down his body and stomped on the side of his face. He was barely conscious and barely breathing after that.

Again, the huge shape was on her, kneeling over her and strangling her with one hand while it pounded her in the face with its other fist, over and over.

With nearly blinding horror he heard the monster's hideous screams, "I OWN you, you cunt! I will NOT allow this! Never again – I'm STOPPING you – you're DEAD!"

Carey Walsh woke up. Mercifully awake but quiet, he lay still for a moment, recovering. He slowly sat up in bed in Lonnie McAllister's Quayville apartment. Beside him, Lonnie stirred and turned toward him.

Saying, "You sound out of breath. What's wrong?" Lonnie reached up and rubbed Carey's shoulder.

"Bad dream," Carey answered in a whisper.

"Same one?" asked Lonnie. Over the years, this had happened before.

When Carey would not elaborate, Lonnie asked him, "Do you want comforting?"

"Yes," Carey answered, "I want comforting. I need comforting."

Carey lay down, facing Lonnie and they kissed, tenderly at first. When their kisses became more passionate, Carey hesitated with his returns but did not pull back away from Lonnie. Lonnie slowed his affection for a moment, then resumed, and they kissed again.

When finally, they moved their bodies against each other, it was Carey's hand on Lonnie's back that moved them.

Chapter 12: The Phantom Vision

Muriel and Nadina began confiding in each other, with Muriel mostly listening, and Nadina doing more of the confiding. Although she said less, since she was the catalyst in this effort, Muriel had bravely opened their friendship up to more sharing of personal details than she herself was used to.

After Muriel told Nadina about meeting Charlie Miller at Marchman Novelties Shop, they began discussing Nadina's 'gentleman caller' and other residents of Mossmead Hamlet. This usually happened during their play dates with Blinky the cat on Thursday late afternoons.

"Thanks for coming out to Charlie's car with me last night, Muriel. He doesn't come inside to greet me or anything because a couple of the boarders, namely Peggy and Tom, don't approve of him or either of us really, and Charlie doesn't like that. Trudy pretty much defends me if they say anything so they won't talk against me for fear of making her mad. But Charlie doesn't live here, so…" Nadina stopped talking and sighed.

"Why don't they approve of you or Charlie?" Muriel asked, mystified.

"It's my fault really, him by association with me. I used to be on the game," Nadina admitted.

Muriel's countenance conveyed she did not get it.

"Um, I sold myself to men for their pleasure. Or rather, Ted sold me. Me and my friends Almalene and Kimberly, we all waited tables and the bar at Ted's tavern. Or inn, as he liked to call it, even though it was really just a bar. He did rent rooms there, but only for an hour or two, mostly just ten to twenty minutes but the guys had to pay for an hour minimum," Nadina giggled about the time limit.

Nadina checked Muriel's expression which registered as sad and perplexed.

Nadina went on, "This was a long, long time ago, Muriel."

"Twenty-some years?" Muriel asked.

"Much longer, over thirty years for me and Almalene. Kim joined in later, maybe just a few months before the whole thing folded, so yeah, for her, around twenty-two, twenty-three years. She was only a teenager then. When Ted bought the building and started business, Almalene was at least late-twenties and I was twenty-four. I'm over 50 years old, Muriel!" Nadina shrugged her shoulders and laughed.

"You look and seem younger, Deena, but that's still young to me. I'm 67, soon a year older," commented Muriel.

"And Giselle is no spring chicken! Don't tell her I told you that. Imagine, all these ancient waitresses at the diner! No wonder baby Kay is so sassy! Boy oh boy, is it a good thing that Ted's gone, out of Mossmead. If he saw Kay the way she is now – whoopee! He was a real humdinger, Ted was. Know what he called that bar of his? Get this, Ye Old Inn!" Nadina started laughing again and Muriel joined in.

"How stupid is that name, huh? We used to laugh so much at that, us girls, I mean. Almalene used to say, like she was talking to men customers, 'Belt a few down, and stick it in – at Ye Old Inn!' Ted even laughed at that. Kim didn't like that much, but she laughed in spite of herself. Kimberly was pretty green-broke for the first month or so. Ted had to re-train her.

"This one time was pretty funny. I was upstairs in a room, the 'ahem' rooms were all upstairs and the bar downstairs. Anyway, I had just taken a guy into a room and from down the hall, in another room with the door open also, came the sound of glass breaking. And then we heard Kim screaming really loud, 'You want me to WHAT?' Then, footsteps running down the hall away from her room, so I looked out into the hall and Kim was standing in front of an open door. She was completely naked and pissed as hell. You've seen Kim, right? Imagine a guy seeing her naked and running away from her! Too damn funny."

Nadina was laughing again but Muriel was at a complete loss for words. She did manage a smile.

Nadina went on, "The good thing about Ted though, he made the johns wear condoms. That damn Marchman, he was a real problem for Ted. For us girls, too, he didn't want to wear rubbers, plus he was too big to be so rough. Kim refused him, and Ted backed her up. Marchman wouldn't pay Almalene cause of she was his wife and he could screw her for free, so I had to take him. But I could handle it though. I'd pretend I was a sheep being ravished by a big old bear, but he made me sore and then he tried to take his money back. He and Ted hated each other on sight."

Muriel asked, "Almalene was … on the game, even though she was married?"

"Yeah, her asshole of a husband slapped her around because she was turning tricks for Ted, but he insisted she work for Ted and screw guys for money because they needed the cash since his shop wasn't making money and they had a kid. That's how come they got married. Almalene was turning tricks in a town east of here, and Marchman wouldn't wear a rubber and she got pregnant so he forced her to marry him. Then they moved here and Ted's bar was right next door."

"I'm sorry, Nadina. Did Charlie buy the shop from Mr. Marchman?"

"No, he kind of inherited it. The big bruiser's name was Marchman Miller. Charlie is his son, his and Almalene's. Now Almalene's gone, Marchman disappeared and Ted left town when his tavern burned to the ground. Kim and I would have been homeless but I went with Charlie, he pays my board, and Kim went to live with Carey Walsh."

Nadina giggled and shimmied her shoulders and squinted at Muriel's face.

She said to Muriel, "Have to say, Harold Carter Walsh, Jr., you know him as Carey, was our best customer! All three of us. I think Almalene was practically in love with him. She wouldn't always charge him; course, part of that could have been cause of how mad that made Marchman when she told him about it. Carey paid her anyway but she only told me that. I miss Almalene, she used to be my best friend."

"Did she disappear along with her husband?" Muriel wanted to understand. "Did they abandon Charlie?"

"No, Charlie was already grown, he was 18 years old when he was left on his own. He had a place for himself set up in the shop building by that time. Thank God, Marchman has never been seen again. But all that was long ago. You're my best friend now, Muriel. I hope you don't mind I told you about all that."

Muriel said, "I'm glad you told me. I'm wondering about so many things. Who is the woman in the picture in Charlie's shop, one of the photographs behind the counter? Do you know?"

"That's Charlie's mother. That was Almalene Lydington Miller."

****

On her next trip to Marchman Novelties, Muriel was

just as intrigued and intimidated as she had been the first time she went there.

After she crossed the bridge Muriel followed the brick walkway around the side of the building. She felt like she was trespassing but she wanted to see where the path led to. Shortly she would regret her curiosity.

Following the path alongside the stone building and past the one car parked on the lot, Muriel walked all the way along the side and across the back, and then around the corner to the vision of a square wooden balustraded balcony, high on the building near the backend of the shop's other side. Attached to the balcony was the top half of a rickety wooden staircase.

Muriel staggered and gasped out loud. Her knees buckled and she almost fell. The visual impact of that paint-chipped truncated stairway hanging from the second story back porch sent waves of chill through Muriel. High above Muriel's head, way more than fifteen feet from the ground, the staircase had been completely chopped off. All stairs from short of midway to the ground were gone.

Hanging suspended due to attachment to the little porch, the old chopped-off paint-chipped white steps and bannisters swayed slightly in the breeze like a barely visible ghost clinging to an earthly haunt it treasured. Or required.

When her vision drifted to the closed wooden second-floor entrance door to or from the balcony, Muriel nearly fainted. No choice, trapped in or shut out. Too high to jump up, too far to fall down. And why?

Cautiously, Muriel turned away from the sight. For a moment she bent her knees, placing her hands on her thighs and lowering her head to let blood run back. When she straightened up, she waited until she could catch her breath, then walked shakily back to the shop entrance and went in.

Charlie was behind the counter waiting on a couple Muriel had not seen before. The man was paying for their purchases but Charlie glanced at Muriel's face and put up a hand and spoke a request to ask the gentleman to wait.

"One moment, please sir. This is one of my buyers; we have a consult meeting coming up. Muriel, if you'll just come over behind the counter and sit down for a moment, I'll get back to you in a few minutes. Thank you."

Charlie opened the swing door in the front of the counter so Muriel could walk a shorter distance to the chair, and she did. He kept wary eyes on her until she managed to be seated, then he accepted money handed to him again, rang up the sale, gave them a receipt, and wished the couple well as they left the shop.

Standing in front of Muriel, Charlie said, "Do you realize how pale your face is? Are you alright?"

"I saw the stairs," she squeaked, trembling a bit.

"I see," Charlie said evenly. "How about a touch of Brandy for you?"

"No, thank you, Charlie. A drink of water, please?"

"Water, then. Coming right up."

Charlie departed through the door between the photographs on the wall and the chair Muriel sat in. He closed the door behind himself. Muriel was terrified that he was angry with her for going where she was not invited, and she wouldn't blame him if he was.

When Charlie returned, he handed her a glass of water and slowly shook his head.

"I should have got rid of that mess a long time ago. No reason to leave that hanging there, none at all. I guess I just couldn't face dealing with it, you know. Hardly anybody goes back there and sees that thing. I'm sorry you did. Shall I tell you how that happened?"

Muriel sipped her water and weakly nodded yes.

"There used to be a tavern on the property next door, only yards from this shop. My father hated Ted Dubbock, the man who owned it, and hated that my mother worked there sometimes and liked to drink there often. Nevertheless, my father stopped there for a beer just about every night after he closed the shop.

"He'd come home after a couple of beers, but Almalene, my mother, wouldn't usually come home with him. She'd stay late drinking, often with men other than my father. He'd sit in the shop on the ground floor and wait for her to come home so he could yell at her and slap her around, so she would use those stairs to the second floor to avoid him. That would burn him even more. By the time he left the shop and went up the inside stairs, she'd already be asleep, or more likely, passed out in bed."

Listening, Muriel sat very still, holding her glass of water, and tried to conceal her dismay. Charlie used his voice softly and calmly, like he was telling a fictional story, but this made his words all the more effective and made Muriel sadder than if he had cried or spoken louder. He must have seen the misery in her face though, because he apologized.

"Sorry so long and … awful, but it gets worse. Finally, he got the idea of shutting off her escape route, so he stood on the lower steps and chopped the stairway apart by swinging an ax over his head. He was 6'5, and he did it in a big-ass fury. He told me all that. Sorry. Stupid as he was, he thought he'd solved the problem.

"So, after a few Friday and Saturday nights of coming home through the front door and facing her maniac husband, Almalene figures she can outfox him. And she kind of does. She doesn't come home until 2 A.M. or later so Marchman has to either stay up all night waiting, or he goes to bed without her or he passes out while sitting in a chair in the shop and she sneaks past him. At any rate, he's too wasted to care, or too frustrated to do much about it."

Charlie looked down at the floor and shuffled his feet, then he looked up into Muriel's eyes again.

"Maybe I leave that broken staircase hang there to remind myself that some people should never marry and never have children. I mean I wouldn't be here if they hadn't but my parents should have never met. And definitely never married each other; it was a union of hatred. I should never marry anyone either, and I won't.

"Deena is the only person who gets next to me physically or otherwise. But I'd like to think I have a friend in Carey and Kim and your landlady and you. I'm sorry you were frightened, Muriel. Is there anything I can do to help?"

"No, thanks, Charlie, I'm fine. I think I'll browse in your shop and buy something to take back to my room."

Aware she had tears in her eyes, Muriel whispered, "Your shop is not a place of hatred, Charlie. I feel comfort and kindness here. I'm glad the shop belongs to you now, and I hope I'll always be your friend."

Charlie nodded his thanks and helped Muriel stand up. Returning the empty glass to him, she moved slowly through the aisles of novelties and found a treasure.

When she set the little iron bulldog on top of the counter, Charlie tore off a small sheet of kitten-and-cat print paper and wrapped it. But he did not hand it to her or tell her the price. He carried the wrapped figurine around the counter, walked to Muriel's side and placed it into her cloth bag.

Lightly pressing her hands holding the straps of her handbag together, Charlie said to her, "Good choice."

After they nodded to each other, Charlie turned away and went through the door behind the counter and Muriel left the shop.

This time she crossed the bridge and headed toward the boarding house without looking back.

Chapter 13: A Festival of Dancing

Friday April 12, one week and one day before the start of spring, began as a tough day for Muriel. Kay O'Shaughnessy had taken vacation starting the day before and would not return to work until after Easter Monday, April 15th. Muriel had to deal with what Before staff called the 'Silas' group, plus waiting on all tables and booths by herself until 11am, starting this day and continuing through Kay's last day of vacation.

Since this included Easter Sunday, and naturally the diner was open and did big business on every holiday, Muriel was needed at work on that Sunday, so she'd have to wash and dry Sunday breakfast dishes at Mrs. V's after she got off work, having just forgone big breakfast and waitressed an extra day. The mere thought of all of this made her Friday all the more challenging.

The moment Muriel approached the Silas group's table, the teasing banter commenced.

"Here she is, boys, our sweet girl, bearing menus," Melvin's singsong greeted her before she could hand out menus or say a word.

Gus cut in instantly, "Why bother us with menus, girly? Didn't Kay have you memorize our orders? She always knows what we want."

Muriel felt her face getting flushed, but she forced herself to stay calm and hand out menus anyhow.

"Kay and I agreed to test you guys, find out if you can read menus and get your own orders right," Muriel sassed them back. "We also agreed that I should do the testing since Kay's too nice."

They all laughed; Muriel could tell that Melvin especially appreciated her initial foray into sarcasm. She could do this; she had an ally. She needed one.

Gus ran a finger quickly down through the breakfast items on one page of his menu, tossed the menu at her, folded his arms and gave her his order rapid-fire, which she dutifully wrote down as fast as she could.

Melvin said, "Gus wants a menu with more pictures," and politely at normal speed told Muriel what he wanted besides coffee. Immediately after, Bert senior mumbled his order at her; luckily, she knew the menu well enough to know how to write up his choices.

While the others ordered, Silas held his menu lowered so he could watch Muriel's face the entire time. Aware of his constant gaze and finding him disarmingly handsome and intimidating, Muriel dared not look at him until he was the last to order. When she focused on his face, she saw the challenge in his brown eyes and his bemused grin.

"Any chance," he said in that quietly authoritative, currently flirtatious voice of his, "I could get you to put a little bourbon in my coffee?"

"I'm sorry, Silas, this diner does not serve booze to

underage people," Muriel answered, knowing by his short rather stylish gray hair and from being told by Kay, that he was over sixty, close to her own age.

Big laughter round the booth this time, but Muriel regretted her answer since he may think she was flirting back.

"They don't serve booze to anyone. Do they, Muriel?" Melvin helped her out.

"Exactly. Thank you, Melvin. They do not." Muriel noticed Silas' grin spreading, to her regret.

Gus said, "Well, well, Muriel. If you were as cute as Kay, you'd be our second favorite waitress."

Surprising herself, Muriel retorted, "If, at my age, I was as cute as Kay, I'd be in big trouble!"

Cutting through the laughter, Silas said, "And if you were our second favorite waitress, you'd be horrified. Right, Muriel?"

"Absolutely, but may I have your order please? Even if I'm your least favorite waitress."

His warm brown eyes grown cold, Silas all but sneered a command to her, "Why don't you come over next to where I'm sitting? I would like to point out my choices to you to be sure you get my order correct."

Muriel did not hesitate, she said to him, "Since you are sitting in a booth, I will take your order from here and then read it back to you so you can verify that it's right."

Melvin said, "She's got your number," a second before Silas began reciting what he wanted for breakfast. He spoke excruciatingly slowly and pronounced each word with such precise crispness that Muriel was mortified. But she read his order back correctly and left their booth.

As she turned her back to them, she heard in gravelly tones from Gus, "Way to go, Si. You fixed her wagon. Wait till she has to take our orders tomorrow!"

But, walking away, Muriel also heard Melvin saying, "Could you give Muriel a break, guys? Land o' livin! Do you have to razz everybody? Especially somebody who's helping you out; doesn't make sense to me."

By the time she was midway between their booth and the counter's closest end, Muriel was playing Kay's voice in her mind saying, 'Never mind them, Sis. They'll shut up once they've got their grub.' It helped, yet heat invaded her face and moisture flooded her eyes.

After she put their orders up for kitchen staff, but before she passed the counter area, Muriel was surprised to feel Giselle's hand on her arm, stopping her.

Guiding Muriel to the far side of the counter, Giselle

hurriedly whispered to her, "Did Trudy ever tell you that Donette Reynolds, Trudy's sister Veronica's oldest girl, walked out of this diner and quit on the spot after waiting on them for the first time? Or have you ever seen Carey Walsh inside this diner?"

"No, never, either one," murmured Muriel.

"You never will see Carey at Before's, ever since one time, close to twenty-one years ago, when Carey and Hal were eating breakfast in here and that bunch started in with their 'if only the mule' business. Carey left food on his plate and walked out of here and never came back. On that day, his daddy stood up and gave them hell for real. Even Gus was quiet. But Hal eats here often, and every time he does, if they're here, he gives them a look that could drop a herd of jackasses, which except for Melvin, is what they are."

"Why are they so mean?" asked Muriel, pondering the fact that Giselle seldom spoke to her, until now.

"No reason except they enjoy being mean," Giselle said, continuing to keep her voice low. "Bert senior has a wife and family at home; Gus has a wife at home, and a son and daughter who both lit out of Mossmead at their first opportunity. *Silas* has a wife and a son; Mac is divorced, probably why he's still working and doesn't come in as often. Melvin is a widower, no children; he's lonely is why he sits with them. After they chased Carey Walsh out of here, Melvin sat at the counter for two months, but he went back when Silas and Gus wouldn't leave him alone."

Muriel whispered quickly, "Thanks, Giselle. Kay never told me any of this."

"She likes them. Which is completely beyond me. Believe you me, I've worked this diner for over 30 years, and I would never, and will never, wait on anybody who doesn't sit at the counter. Promise me, you won't let them make you quit. The rest of the staff would commit mass suicide if that happened."

Tears receded as Muriel smiled and hugged Giselle while whispering her 'thanks' in Giselle's ear.

When Muriel delivered breakfast orders to the 'Silas' booth, not one word was said by anyone. However, Muriel adroitly and deliberately gave Melvin extra coffee. And a promptly returned thank-you nod.

****

Next day, Saturday, after another taxing shift Muriel was heading for late lunch with Hal Walsh when a cheerful Trudy V entered the diner and hooked arms with Muriel before she could sit down in Hal's booth.

"Excuse me, dears," said Trudy, "but I'm proposing an Easter weekend switch of lunch dates. If Miss Muriel will have lunch with me today since I have things, I need to speak with her about, would you mind postponing your lunch with Muriel until Easter Monday, Hal?"

Hal smiled at both ladies. "Not as long as I've got Monday lunch promised to me. Muriel?"

Muriel responded to Hal, "Absolutely, Monday is yours next week.   Change back on the following week though?" she asked both of them.

"Of course, of course. I'm spending Easter Sunday and Monday with family in Quayville, in fact, I'm on my way after cooking breakfast tomorrow, which is why we need to talk, Muriel. I've put Reed and Nadina in charge of the boarding house since I know you and Turner would not want to be in charge and Peggy or Tom would." Trudy kept hold of Muriel's arm while smiling at Hal.

"Thank you, Hal, I do appreciate your letting me borrow your lunch date. I need to make sure Muriel is prepared to attend the church social next week on Saturday the 20th," Trudy gave a conspiring smile to Hal, then steered Muriel to their usual lunch booth on the other side of the diner.

After she and Trudy sat down and ordered from Nadina, Muriel asked her lunch companion, "Church social?"

Trudy said, "We'll get back to that. First, details about tomorrow.   Reed and Deena are going to set up breakfast on the side board early so churchgoers can attend, and if she has time, Deena will clear the dishes and rinse them. Then, after your shift here at the diner, if you don't mind, you can wash and dry dishes and put them away. Sunday lunch and supper will be fix-your-own sandwiches or soup, and Monday breakfast will be cereal and coffee as long as you, Deena, and Reed don't mind making soup and coffee. You three will get extra credit, paid in cash by me when I return on Monday afternoon. You needed to hear all that, but Hal didn't."

Seeing Nadina bringing their food to the booth, Trudy informed Muriel, "We'll talk about the church social while we eat."

They did. Mrs. V started with, "The social is held every spring at the church Peggy, Reed and Tom belong to, Mossmead Hamlet Lutheran Church, the only place of worship located here in town. You know where it is, the building with the spire. But the social doesn't take place in the church proper, instead it's in the room where Sunday school is taught. A large room with tables and chairs that get pushed back to create a dance floor."

At the words 'dance floor' Muriel's perception of church social perked up.

Trudy went on, "Peggy Little and the other church ladies make sure that everyone in town is invited, even me, Turner, you and Deena, everyone. They feel that having major league attendance at the festive social may encourage a soul or two to join the church. And Peggy has assured me with great enthusiasm that it works. It starts around 5pm and goes until 11 or so, and there is free food and some kind of punch to drink, and music. Not just church music, either.

"I will drive you, Turner and Nadina to the church so we can all dress up a little. You should know that even Hal and Carey Walsh attend this "to-do" every year," noting Muriel's expression at the mention of Hal's and Carey's names, Trudy's eyes sparkled with glee.

"Now I always bring more than a few homecooked dishes and everyone from our boarding house will be there, so our Saturday supper will be held at the church. This happens every year but it's your first time, and I must warn you that everyone, and that does mean everyone, in Mossmead attends," with this statement, Trudy looked straight into Muriel's eyes.

Muriel asked, "Does Charlie Miller go to the social?"

Smiling and shaking her head Trudy had her own question.

"Dear child, does that mind of yours ever rest? You do have it figured. No, Charlie is the exception. He does not attend the social and never has. I personally believe he does afterhours business every Saturday night. Something mysterious, maybe something naughty."

"Afterhours business?"

"Yes, ma'am, I think so. Late one Saturday night my momma had to go to the hospital in Quayville and my sister Veronica picked me up in her husband's car so we could help momma and be with papa, and on the way, we drove past Charlie's shop after it was closed. "Now, it was dark all around the front but we saw three or four cars in the back of the parking lot. And Mr. Charlie makes more money than his daddy did; that's for sure."

Muriel paid rapt attention to the mashed potatoes in her lunch as she feared Trudy Vinterbos might somehow be able to read in her eyes what she was thinking about. The erotic image of Carey Walsh on the front of the black-and-white photo card had appeared in Muriel's mind after she heard the words 'afterhours business.'

She heard Trudy saying, "Never mind that though, Charlie won't be there at the church, which is why it's good Carey Walsh always dances with Deena. You might be interested to know, Miss Muriel, that Carey dances with all the ladies. And he is quite the dancer, my dear. Do you like to dance?"

When Muriel looked up, Trudy was grinning and peering at her.

"Yes, I do like to dance, Trudy. But it's been a long, long time since I've danced with anybody."

"All the more reason to come to the social and catch up with your dancing! That is settled then. Excellent. After lunch would you like to join me in my car for a trip to the chicken farm to check in with Charlotte?"

"Yes please, I would," sighed Muriel, making her landlady happy and setting off a case of fluttering nerves in herself. Only one week until the church social.

****

With the ladies Trudy, Nadina and Muriel wearing their best dresses, or in Muriel's case, only dress, and Turner verging on elegance in his pale blue suit, they determined to arrive at the church early to get a parking space on the lot. Trudy was at the wheel, Deena and Muriel sat in back and the front passenger seat was reserved for Turner who worked his way slowly down the porch steps and over sidewalk to Trudy's car, parked in front of the boarding house.

Turner always moved slowly, Muriel had noticed this from her arrival, and knew the reason because he explained to her during early days.

"Arthritis," Turner had mentioned to her, "In my back, my shoulders and elbows and knees. I'm a broke man, Muriel, in more ways than one. Doc Bailey, only doctor in Mossmead, said I'm too tall to work as hard as I did at being a janitor and a waiter. Said my bones objected. Imagine what good it did me to hear that."

"None, I would guess," Muriel had answered him.

"Correct. You guess right," Mr. Stanhope had agreed.

Fortunately, on this night of the social, Trudy and pals

arrived in time to park close to the classroom, a long portion of the building behind the church proper. This allowed Turner a shorter walk before he could sit at Trudy's table inside. Trudy carried a large rectangular pan with one of her supper contributions in it, and Muriel and Nadina carried additional food containers, plus they took two trips each to go back for more. Peggy greeted them all while she put food containers in order and stacked paper plates and cups and plastic silverware on long tables against the wall at the side of the room near the entrance door.

Meanwhile Trudy and Turner had commandeered one of the longest tables and Muriel saw, with tremendous relief, that a seat at one end, and one empty seat away from where Turner sat, was saved for her. After squeezing Muriel's hand Nadina passed that table to sit at and save a small table in a corner area separated from the main seating. As she left Muriel's side, she explained.

"I would sit with you guys, Muriel, but I always sit with Kim and Carey at these things. Hope you don't mind?"

"Of course not, Deena," came the answer from one who knew she most likely could not eat if she sat at the same table as Carey Walsh.

Shortly, the Medley family joined Trudy, Turner and Muriel at their table. Charlotte, Clark and kids Alphonse and Hazel, plus Clark's uncle Paul Medley, who was second-shift chief cook at the Before the

Highway Diner, extended warm greetings with the three already seated.

Lightly squeezing Muriel's shoulders, Charlotte bent down a little to admire the one fancy dress Muriel owned.

"Look at you, so pretty, Muriel!" Charlotte said.

"And you, Charlotte! You and your dress are lovely," was Muriel's apt description of Charlotte's knee-length short-sleeved lacy white dress decorated with roses printed in red. And how Charlotte looked in it.

"Thanks, always a shock to see me in civilian clothes!" laughed Charlotte before she turned to admire Turner's suit and Trudy's outfit.

Hazel twirled around full-circle beside Muriel's chair and chirped, "Don't I look pretty? And look at Alphonse – he has a checkered bowtie!"

Muriel said, "Beautiful and handsome! I'm blown away."

"Muriel said a current thing!" exclaimed Alphonse, making his eyes wide. "Far out! Now we have to thank Trudy and Turner for scoring the best table, closest to the food."

Trudy laughed as she turned in her chair and opened her arms for both children, and they scurried over to her.

Turner chuckled when he said to Muriel, "You go over to get your food by table and this one is always first. We sit here every year and every year Peggy is tempted to start at the other end. She tries to hide it but you can see it in her face."

Muriel glanced at Peggy's face and giggled. "I feel lucky. And there's also dancing, is there?"

"After we eat. Some people dance and most others watch. I'm a watcher myself. Used to dance but not anymore. After a bit Reed will bring his record player in, and then he, Carey Walsh, Antoine and others will start asking ladies to dance. Do you dance, Muriel?"

"Yes, if someone asks me."

"Someone will ask. If not any adults, I'm pretty sure Alphonse might."

Gleefully, Muriel said, "I would adore dancing with Alphonse!"

"After you see him dance, I mean, he can move to the beat but he looks pretty silly doing it, you probably gonna change your mind."

The tables were filling with Mossmead residents, some Muriel knew as acquaintances or as customers from the diner, and some she didn't know. The room was becoming crowded with people and Muriel was getting nervous. Nadina still sat alone at her small table.

Muriel was about to go over to Nadina's table to talk with her when she saw Hal and Carey Walsh and Kim Hodges walk into the room. As she watched Carey and Kim approach Nadina's table, Muriel was surprised to notice that although Carey wore a suit and tie, Kim dressed down in short-sleeved cotton blouse and denim jeans with flats.

Hal appeared casual but sporty in colorful Hawaiian shirt and beige trousers. After he and Carey took their food contributions to the table Peggy presided over, Hal came over to the first table in line, pulled out the empty chair between Turner and Muriel and sat down. Even behind his wireframe spectacles, Hal's eyes were smiling.

"You look gorgeous tonight," Hal said to Muriel. Then, turning his face the other way, "You too, Turner."

"Thank you, I love your shirt," Muriel told Hal, while Turner muttered, "Thanks, man, I guess."

During suppertime Muriel enjoyed listening to happy chatter, mostly provided by Trudy Vinterbos and Charlotte Medley with additions and interludes by Clark and Paul, and occasionally Hal or Alphonse. Hazel kept up a running commentary on various dishes she tasted, such as, "Them sweet potatoes – *good*," or "Don't care for green beans in weird sauce."

As general conversation died down after dessert with coffee, tea or hot chocolate, Muriel noticed Reed and Carey setting up a record player in a corner, and each carrying a speaker toward and pointing to the center of the room's open space. She also saw two boxes, one nearly filled with 33-size records, the other with 45s, sitting on a foldup table positioned near the corner; Reed and Carey were talking while going through records and setting some aside.

Muriel wondered if Carey would dance first with Kim, and she glanced at their small table where Kim was lighting a cigarette. Seconds later, Peggy Little bustled over to Kim and began an animated discussion, at least on Peggy's part. Kim rolled her eyes, shook her head, and finally stubbed out her cigarette in her coffee cup. Peggy returned to her own table to sit with her senior parents, and her brother, his wife and their kids.

Turner leaned in back of Hal to tell Muriel, "There's no smoking in the church building and Kim knows that. But she tries to get away with it every time. And every time, Peggy don't let her."

Muriel hated to ask but felt she had to, so she turned to Hal and said, "Does Kim smoke in their apartment above the barn?"

"No," Hal answered in a firm tone of voice. "Carey won't let her and I won't let her. She goes outside to smoke beside the diner and stands on the pavement and carries an ashtray with her. She feels put-upon, but it's too darn bad. No smoking near a barn, ever."

Reassured, Muriel then asked, "Will Carey dance with Kim first?"

Again, Hal said no, then Turner spoke, "Kim don't dance."

"Never?" asked Muriel. "Not with anybody?"

Hal said, "That's right. I've heard her say that she's danced with enough men for a lifetime; she's sick of it and she won't dance again. Period."

Reed put a record on, music started playing, and Reed took Peggy while Carey took Nadina out to the dance floor. From across the room handsome Antoine Alford, Before Diner's morning shift sous chef, stood up from a table seating Giselle Varner and her husband, also young Destry Burton, plus Kay O'Shaughnessy and her date Deputy Alex Keyton.

Antoine walked across the dance floor to Trudy Vinterbos and asked her for a dance. Trudy laughed and told him she was too old for him, but Antoine persisted and soon they were out on the floor, dancing along with other couples, some Muriel didn't recognize.

Watching the dancers along with Hal, Turner, and the Medleys, Muriel could see that while Reed and Carey looked like good dance partners for their ladies, Antoine was a superb mover. Trudy managed to keep up with him, but Muriel wasn't sure she could. Yet she knew she wouldn't turn him down if he asked.

The next song was a ballad, a slow dance. To Muriel's surprise, Carey chose Peggy as his partner. Reed danced with his mother, while Nadina, Trudy, and Antoine sat out the dance. Clark and Charlotte Medley danced close together and everyone currently seated at their table watched them.

Hal whispered to Muriel, "If I could dance, I'd ask you, but I'm worse than two left feet. We'd both be tortured."

Muriel smiled at him, "I'm enjoying watching the dancing and listening to the music, but thanks for saying that."

Looking past Muriel, Hal said, "Don't think I had to."

When Muriel turned her face away from Hal, she saw Carey standing next to her chair and smiling while he held out his hand in her direction.

"Hey, Muriel, would you like to dance with me?"

"Sure," she heard herself say, as though in a trance.

Every inch of her skin seemed to be buzzing with nerves when Muriel took Carey's hand and walked out on the dance floor with him. Eydie Gorme's hit record "Blame It on the Bossa Nova," dancing music with a faster rhythm, began to play.

"Do you know the bossa nova?" Carey asked Muriel.

"Um, no. I'll try, but I don't do fancy," was her answer.

"That's fine, I'll show you, and I don't do fancy either. Follow me," Carey said.

After a tentative beginning, they got into rhythm with each other, and Muriel let go somewhat. She had to remind herself to breathe, though. In all her life, she had never thought she would be dancing with a man she was hopelessly attracted to. And having fun doing it. Especially since Carey seemed to enjoy dancing with her, plus he was kind to her.

When their dance ended and they nodded thanks to each other, then walked in different directions, Muriel kept saying silently to herself, 'It's been a dream, even if it never happens again. A dream.'

A huge smile decorated her face when she reached her place at the table and Hal stood and pulled her chair out for her.

"I think you like dancing," Hal told her.

"Yes," Muriel said with spirit.

"That's good, because he'll ask again, I'm sure."

As soon as he said that, and a ballad began to play, Muriel was asked to dance by Reed Mosgrove. She nodded to Reed, smiled at Hal, and got back up for another dance. Slow dancing with Reed was easy for her; he was a friend she could relax with. She knew she was too old for Reed as well as for Carey, but with Reed, she didn't care. A dance was a dance and she was grateful to be asked again.

Although Muriel did get to dance quite a few times, including again with Carey and Reed, once each with Antoine, Paul Medley, and even with Melvin Howard, she also adored sitting at the table and listening to the music.

When Muriel lived with her parents, she listened to recordings of the music they loved, mostly jazz and big band sounds, like Duke Ellington and Glenn Miller. At the dress factory where she had worked any piped-in tunes playing were exclusively country music, which Muriel also liked but not exclusively.

On this night at the church social Muriel danced and listened to popular songs, some she had already heard playing on the radio in Mrs. V's kitchen; for instance, "Ramblin' Rose" by Nat King Cole, "Strangers in the Night" by Frank Sinatra, and The Supremes' "You Can't Hurry Love."

At the start of a song with country flavor and one that Muriel had heard before and really liked, "Only the Lonely" by Roy Orbison, she observed Carey and Nadina's slow dance together. They held each other very close, their arms around each other's waists, Deena's cheek resting on Carey's shoulder.

During that Roy Orbison ballad, Reed had asked Trudy to dance but she turned him down in her inimitable style, giving those seated at their table a laugh.

"I can't dance with you, son – you're one of my boarders! If ever I have to throw you out for non-payment, you're going to give me grief, saying 'well, you enjoyed dancing with me, didn't you, and now you're going to toss me out like last night's garbage!' I can't be putting myself in for that kind of logic, now, can I?"

Reed chuckled and shrugged his shoulders and said, "Well then, who am I going to dance with?"

"Muriel's free. Peggy's free. I'm not stopping you from dancing with other boarders, just not me, the big bad boss! My goodness!"

Muriel stood up when Reed looked at her and they walked out on the floor, but by then the music had changed to a number Muriel was completely unfamiliar with. Clark Medley had played Chubby Checker's "The Twist," and some dancers hurried to leave the floor. Deena among them.

Standing still and staring at Reed who was laughing, blushing and attempting to dance, all at the same time, Muriel just shook her head in confusion. She was vaguely aware of Carey and Kay beginning to dance a little distance from Reed, who kept cracking up.

Antoine had outrun Clark to Charlotte's side and was leading her out on the floor while he apologized to her husband. But Clark told Antoine he'd rather watch than dance so go ahead, and Charlotte seemed thrilled.

Watching Reed's movements to try and imitate them, Muriel was laughing almost as much as he was. Then she glanced at Antoine and Charlotte to behold a different rhythm and sexy fluid style, not nearly as awkward as what she and Reed were attempting. Carey Walsh's easy hip movements were closer to Antoine's than to Reed's, while his partner Kay improvised arm and hand motions that looked like fun.

Muriel knew she couldn't move as sensually as the other couples, so she went back to following Reed's twisting style and laughing throughout the dance. As the record ended, she couldn't help glancing Carey's way. Kay threw her arms around Carey and said something to him, causing him to tilt his head back and roar with laughter and bringing Muriel to sizzle with jealousy during her walk back to the table.

Instead of sitting down Muriel grabbed her beverage cup and walked over to the food and drinks table for a non-alcoholic punch refill. By doing this, she avoided being asked to dance and she gratefully returned to her seat to sip her drink and listen to the music.

Dusty Springfield's "You Don't Have to Say You Love Me" was playing and for a moment Muriel watched Kay and her date two-stepping to the music. Reed and Peggy were dancing also, but Carey was not on the dance floor. He was talking with Kim and Deena at their small table.   Kim and Deena laughed and gestured while they spoke, very animated, but Carey, positioned between them, sat back a little. He looked amused but also a little bashful.

During the next record, "Daydream Believer" by The Monkees, Muriel continued to gaze at Carey until a sudden moment when he glanced her way. Their eyes met and just before she turned aside, Carey gave Muriel the sweetest smile.

Afraid her adoration had been obvious; Muriel stared into her punch and rattled the ice around. When she looked up Hal was watching her.

"Did the twist do you in for dancing, Muriel?" Hal asked with a smile.

"Kind of. The twist was fun, but I feel like I've danced enough now. I love listening to this music though."

The music had stopped while she spoke, so Muriel turned to Hal and giggled, but he was watching his son walk across the dance floor to where Reed was sorting through records. Then both Hal and Muriel kept eyes on Carey, but he was too distant and too softspoken for them to hear what he said.

Carey asked Reed, "If I asked you to dance with me, would you?"

Reed pondered that for a couple of beats, then

answered, "Almost," and went back to sorting through records.

Chuckling with delight, Carey put a hand on Reed's shoulder and with his other hand placed a 45-single on the table in front of Reed.

"Play the flip side for me, would you, but wait until I'm out on the floor with a partner who will dance with me."

Reed turned the record over and checked the song title.

"Is this serious?" Reed asked.

"No," said Carey, "but I'd like it to be a little bit nice."

Carey left Reed and walked over to Muriel Dunphy. Muriel watched him approach but was afraid to look up at him when he arrived.

"One more dance, please, Muriel?" Carey cocked his head in her direction to catch her attention.

Knowing she couldn't refuse him Muriel wordlessly lifted her right hand and he gently held her hand. They walked quietly together out to the center of the dance area and Carey positioned them for a slow dance. He asked her if an unfancy waltz was okay and she nodded yes.

And then the song began to play.

Although she had never heard "Don't Worry Baby" by The Beach Boys before, Muriel knew from the start she would never forget this song. The lyrics and Brian Wilson's hauntingly romantic lead vocals, the easy rhythm, the reassuring but stirring sound of the song made Muriel feel she had been waiting all her life to hear this song. And now she was dancing to it.

When they started dancing, Carey held Muriel closer than before, so they barely touched each other. Since his sports jacket was open, she could feel his body beneath his dress shirt. That, and the warmth of his hand holding hers, the happy look in his eyes, and the way they moved smoothly together sent her to paradise.

As they seemed to sail around the dance floor, Muriel imagined she and Carey were flying, not touching ground. She knew she couldn't have him as her own lover, but to have this tender and ecstatic moment would be precious to her forever.

The song ended and he bowed to her curtsey.

Smiling, he said, "Thank you, Miss Muriel. That was a very fine dance."

She put a hand against his chest and leaned toward him to whisper simply, "And thank you, Carey. I loved the song and our dance very much."

That night Muriel slept with her arms around her pillow.

<u>Chapter 14: Interim Moments</u>

In the following week during her regular Friday lunch with Kay, Muriel decided to be more forward than was her custom and ask questions when she was puzzled or curious about something. She started with Kay.

"What did you say to Carey at the church social that made him laugh so hard after you two did the twist?"

Kay raised an eyebrow and screwed her mouth into a funny shape, but she did answer Muriel's question.

"I thanked him for choosing me as his partner for the 'twist' dance since I now knew what it would be like to dance with him horizontally – like in bed with him," as she spoke, Kay observed Muriel's face for her reaction.

Biting her lip, Muriel giggled and said, "You really said that to him?"

"Yep, but no surprise there. As everyone knows, any thought that comes into my head comes out my mouth, most times before I ever really think about it. He took it the right way though. But you know what was kind of awful about that dance, Muriel?"

"Looked like fun, so I do not."

"After I danced with Carey, then danced with my date the deputy, I could tell I may as well pass on having sex with my date. Didn't you get the feeling from even just watching the dance floor that the only guys worth going all the way with were Carey and Antoine? I did, and I'm kind of afraid of really doing it with either of them. Well, also Clark but he's our boss and married besides. And no offense, but Paul Medley and Hal Walsh are too old for me. I was thinking I might never get laid again. If not for Silas' son Mark that is."

"Mark?"

"Yeah, but don't worry, Sis, I'm on the pill. Mark took me to Philly for my vacation. It was pretty boss. I'm thinking he's my best bet for a way out of this nowhere town to life in the city. I'm a city girl at heart, and he's studying for his real estate license, so… But don't say anything, okay, Muriel? It could take a while and I might get tired of him before it happens. So, mum's the word, okay?"

"You've got it, Kay," said Muriel, thinking of this revelation as a doomsday warning.

****

At Saturday's lunch with Hal, Muriel received a question before she could ask any.

"Muriel, about that church social, should I be apologizing for my son? Maybe for encouraging something he can't deliver?" Hal wondered.

"Never," said Muriel.

"That's a relief to hear, but I know you have eyes for him. You, along with Kim Hodges, Lonnie McAllister, some jasper from Quayville named Dale Brand, I think he's a friend of Carey's, Lonnie's, and Charlie's, plus probably our Kay here at Before, possibly Natalie Reynolds, and maybe half the town. You do know about all that?"

Muriel told him, "I do. And I know my feelings for Carey will never be more than a fantasy. But for me, fantasy is enough, no apologies necessary."

Hal winced a little and when he spoke in return, his eyes had the faraway look they sometimes had when he wasn't smiling or listening to something he liked hearing. But his voice was warm.

"Okay, but as long as you're not hurting over this. Carey would never want to hurt you, Muriel. And neither would I."

Muriel said, softly and slowly, "Thank you, but don't worry, Hal, I'm not hurt by Carey or you. I understand."

Now she had questions for Hal Walsh, but they were questions she might never ask.

****

Monday's lunch with Trudy Vinterbos presented opportunities Muriel intended to enjoy.

After they had started eating and Trudy filled Muriel in about her Easter visit with family, Muriel began.

"Trudy, you had a happy marriage, didn't you?"

"Oh Lord, yes, child, we did, Peter Vinterbos and I. Wish it could have been longer, but it was wonderful, just like working for him and his first wife Ethel was wonderful. They came over from Germany, became citizens, had the Victorian house built and hired me as live-in housekeeper. They both treated me like family.

"She was older than he was but they both had money, so after she passed, he asked me to stay on. Around six months later, he started dating a string of ladies but he told me every one of them just wanted him for his money. He said because of that, he could not trust any of them the way he trusted me since we were friends. And we were friends; we could talk about anything. I will always feel that's the best basis for a marriage. When he proposed, I said yes."

Trudy sipped her root beer and peered into Muriel's eyes.

"Are you sure you want to hear all this?"

Nodding emphatically, Muriel said, "I really do, yes." She got a sly look on her face and added, "I have my reasons."

"Nefarious reasons?" Trudy asked, and Muriel nodded again.

"Those are the best kind," said Trudy before continuing. "Peter was older than I was and so much wiser and he was a kind man, and not just to me."

"Do you mind if I ask how old you are, Trudy?"

"Heh heh, mind? No, I don't mind, but I tell everyone the same story. I'm 59 and I've been 59 for numerous years, or longer, but that's my story and I'm sticking to it! I was a lot younger when we married but age difference was not a problem for me. Race difference wasn't either, not for him or for me, but…maybe for others.

"Dare I tell you that my frequent association with white people, married to one, friendly with several, used to alienate me from my family and some of my friends of color. My sister Veronica and I did not speak to each other for over a year. Lucky that changed after I hired two of her daughters, the older two Donette and Elise, to clean for Peter and I, and we paid them well."

"Did your husband will you the house? Am I rude to ask that?"

"No, not rude, dear, and yes, he blessedly left me the house. He and Ethel never had children and he and I had no children, so I got the money and the boarding house. Well, that was my doing, after Peter was gone. Taking in boarders was my idea and I'm glad I did. Can I tell you? I'm secretly glad all of my 'children' have been boarders or cats."

****

The next couple of weeks passed uneventfully while Muriel worked her regular shifts at the Before Diner, spent time at the Walsh home, mostly with Hal and the animals, visited the chicken farm, and kept up with fun playtimes with Blinky the cat in Deena's room.

Weather was delightful on a Sunday midmorning while Muriel washed breakfast dishes and gazed out kitchen windows open to screens. Mrs. V stepped into the kitchen. She wore her standard fancy flowy dress with hat and heels for going to church, and she was humming as she strolled over to Muriel.

"Muriel, dear, would you mind setting out the fixings for Sunday sandwich trays for me? I'm being driven to church and then taken out to lunch in Quayville – at the Riverbank Cafe, no less, so I may be late getting back. I apologize for short notice, I just found out about the lunch from my benefactor Serenity."

'Serenity?' Muriel wondered. She said, "Of course I wouldn't mind and I know exactly what to do. Is it your birthday, Trudy?"

"Oh no, dear, nothing special, just lunch with a friend who drops by for a visit from time to time. She's almost as generous as she is unpredictable, but it's very kind of her to treat me today and I never turn down free food. Especially at Riverbank Cafe."

They could hear the door knocker sounded and footsteps of someone wearing high heels, then the front door opening and ensuing conversation.

Peggy's voice saying, "Oh. Severn Sagal."

A husky voice answered, "Hi, Peg. I'm Serenity today, can't you tell? How about letting me come in. I promise I won't bite you today. I'm saving all my appetites for lunch with Trudy at Cafe Riverbank in Quayville. For Mother's Day, since she's the mom I always wished I had."

In the kitchen, steps were heard going away and steps were heard approaching.

Trudy said, "She's coming back here. I want you to meet her anyway."

The lady who appeared in the kitchen entrance looked to be over six feet tall. She was slender but sinuous in an alluring manner and had long blonde waving hair and a naturally very pretty face. Her bohemian peasant dress, printed in blue-green paisley with ruffled sleeves and hem and worn with high boots, reminded Muriel of hippies she had seen on television and admired.

"Happy Mother's Day, Miss Trudy! I swear, I don't think Peggy likes Serenity nearly as much as we do. But I guess that's as expected. Oh hello, darling lady! I'm Serenity; what's your name? I know I've never met you before."

Trudy spoke sooner, "This is Muriel Dunphy. She is my latest boarder here at Mrs. V's, and she is truly a darling, I'm happy to say. Muriel, even though Miss Serenity is not actually my daughter, she takes me out for Mother's Day every year and I am most appreciative!"

"Lovely to meet you, Miss Serenity," said Muriel.

"Likewise, Miss Muriel," Serenity rejoined, giving a mini curtsey and striding over to beside Muriel.

Although slightly intimidated, Muriel was also fascinated since Serenity moved in a vaguely but sensuously predatory manner and spoke in an unusual offkey timbre, neither of which Muriel had ever experienced before.

Draping a long languid arm around Muriel's shoulders, Serenity raised an eyebrow and spoke in a low voice to her, thoroughly enchanting her.

"While I may be a lady, at times when I choose to, I am decidedly no one's daughter. Except Miss Trudy's, but only in spirit. I was born here in Mossmead Hamlet, Muriel, a little fledgling peeping in a way the natives did not understand before I became a full-blown bird and flew the nest all the way to the Westcoast, where I now live and perform. I only fly back once a year and only for Trudy Vinterbos. May I hope to see you again next year, Muriel? Maybe you'll join us then?"

"I would love that, if I could?" Muriel looked at Trudy.

Trudy answered, "I believe you certainly could and hope you will, and since Mother's Day is celebrated on Sundays, we'll either get someone else to do the dishes or you and I will take care of them later."

"Thanks!" said Muriel.

"Better than perfect," Serenity said and continued, "And since I only perform at night and never on Sunday night, I'll be available next year, too."

"Settled a year in advance," Trudy decided, walking forward to leave the kitchen.

Serenity gave Muriel a hug and stepped over to hook arms with Trudy on their way out.

"We're off!" said Serenity, glancing back over her shoulder at Muriel to add in a deeper voice, "And how!" to Muriel's delighted laughter. And to her delayed realization that underneath her dress, Serenity was male by birth.

<u>Chapter 15: The Telling</u>

On another Sunday but in the afternoon and months after Mother's Day, Muriel ventured into Marchman Novelty Shop again. She wasn't sure exactly why she felt compelled to visit Charlie's shop, but she did. She was inclined to suppose she really didn't want to know the reason.

On the preceding Saturday morning Muriel had awoken shortly before her alarm rang at five. Turning off her alarm she put on her robe and slippers and stood at her window. Although it was still dark, street lights, some lights inside houses, and overhead floodlighting above the center of the trestle bridge to Charlie's shop gave illumination to portions of the scene far outside Muriel's window.

Muriel caught up her breath. Two male figures were standing on the trestle bridge. In light bathing them from above and because of their distinctive silhouettes, Muriel could tell that one was Charlie Miller and the other was Carey Walsh. While she watched, Charlie stretched out one arm and patted Carey on the shoulder and they turned away from each other. Charlie moved back toward Marchman Novelties and Carey walked off the other end of the bridge and into the woods between the canal and the river.

Inside the shop on Sunday, Muriel approached the counter and glanced behind it to find Charlie sitting in his chair against the wall and reading a book. He looked up at her; the bells on the door had rung when she came in. Placing a marker in his book and setting his book on the chair seat after he stood up, Charlie came to the counter across from Muriel.

"Looking for something special, pretty lady?" he asked.

Muriel bit her lips, then answered, "I don't know. I'm so confused, so worried about Carey, Hal, Turner, everyone. So many things here in Mossmead puzzle me. I don't understand things people say or do, and I don't know why I'm bothering you about all this, Charlie. I'm sorry; maybe I should leave?"

"No, stay, Muriel," Charlie told her as he maneuvered out from behind the counter in front and hung a 'Closed' sign on the outside of the front door and shut and locked it. He held the swing section at the front of the counter open and motioned her in.

After they passed through to the rear portion of the high-ceilinged storage room, they came to another door, this one set into what appeared to be the back wall, off to the side nearest to the shop.

"Would you care to join me for hot tea in my apartment back here? I can explain a few things to you, stuff that happened 23 or so years ago. I don't think anyone else in town will tell you. Come on back to my little breakfast nook and we'll have tea and chat, just like actual civilized people."

Muriel nodded to thank him and when he opened the

door, she preceded him inside. While she waited Charlie used a key to lock the door from inside and then he bolted the door shut with a substantial slide bolt. His action caused a sliver of fear to course through Muriel but she managed to ignore it.

Charlie flipped a wall-mounted light switch to illuminate an open kitchenette area near a small square table with two chairs set against the windowless wall. Beyond this open section was a narrow hall with closed doors to rooms lining one side, the same side as the kitchen. Muriel could see that the opposite wall was adorned with a series of separately spaced framed pictures.

She could only see detail in the first picture, the one closest to the apartment's entrance door. It was a black-and-white full-front photograph of Kim Hodges wearing only eye and lip makeup and a short necklace of dark beads and bending forward toward the camera. She had one hand on her left leg thrust forward and she held her other hand a little over waist high, beckoning with a forefinger whoever viewed the photo. Her eyes at half-mast and her chin level, Kim's lips were marginally open with corners turned slightly up.

Seeing this photograph, Muriel had no doubts about the photographer of Carey's picture-card still hidden in her nightstand. Or about Charlie Miller's afterhours business.

"Have a seat, won't you, Muriel," Charlie motioned to

the chair facing toward the kitchenette and waited until Muriel sat down.

"Will English Breakfast Tea suit you?" he asked. "With cream and sugar?"

"Yes, I would love that. Thank you, Charlie. You're taking so much trouble with me."

"About time somebody did, don't you think?" he did not wait for an answer but sauntered over to a small ancient-looking stove and put a kettle of water on one of the electric burners.

An unframed photograph in color was affixed to the wall, above the table, and it captivated Muriel. The inside of a window frame bordered the picture, and through the pictured window a tree-covered hill could be seen, as though the onlooker gazed out a window that wasn't really there.

As Muriel remembered, there were not any windows in the entire ground floor of the building. In addition, the overhead light in the kitchenette area did not fully extend to where the table was positioned, giving a cave-like quality to where Muriel and Charlie sat to talk and drink tea. This encouraged any inclination to cloak an afternoon visit as though it was a telling of secrets in the dead of night.

After they both added cream and sugar and sipped their hot tea, Charlie began to speak using an almost hushed voice with emotional tones suppressed just underneath the surface. His voice reminded Muriel of the way someone would share tales being told around a campfire, tales of long-ago mysterious stories passed on to others throughout the ages so they would never be forgotten.

Charlie opened with, "I'm going to tell you something I never talk about."

His first mention informed her of what she already knew, that the photograph of the woman's face she had previously admired was a portrait of his mother, Almalene.

But then he added, "Over twenty years ago, she was murdered in the woods, just beyond the towpath."

Charlie took a swallow of tea, checked Muriel's face to gage her reaction, and continued in his calm voice.

"It happened very late one Friday night. My mother had gone out drinking at the neighborhood inn with her favorite of the men she was cheating with. When Marchman, my father, closed the shop after ten that night, he went to the inn but she was gone already. He came back to the shop and went upstairs to their flat and when she wasn't home either, he got furious and told me to stay there, downstairs in the shop, and he was going out to find her. I knew that was bad, but I didn't fight him, I just agreed to do what he wanted."

Although Charlie continued to speak in a gentle casual voice, Muriel was transported to a highly emotional, terribly violent scene as his words painted a devastating picture of anger and revenge.

"Hours later, neither my mother or my father returned and I fell asleep on the chair behind the counter. Someone furiously pounding on the front door woke me. I knew the door was locked so I got up and opened it, expecting my miserable parents to come in. But no, it was Carey Walsh, looking like something run over by a truck and left for dead. One of his eyes was swollen shut and his whole face was so battered it seemed caved in.

"Besides that, he couldn't stand up straight, his clothes were torn and covered with dirt, and he was gasping for breath. He barely whispered to me to close and bolt the door shut. I did that and then I had to help him stagger back here to my apartment and sit him in that chair you're in. He managed to ask if I could bolt the door to my apartment, so I did that, too."

As she listened to Charlie's words, Muriel pictured Carey in the condition Charlie described. When Charlie repeated what Carey had told him, Muriel heard Carey's voice speaking to her. For her, it was as though Charlie's tale took her back in time to experience what had happened so many years ago.

She began to lose herself in a dual reality. When Charlie told what happened, Muriel saw Charlie and listened to his tale of horror. But when Charlie repeated what Carey had said, Muriel heard and pictured Carey, exhibiting emotion with every word.

Charlie's words painted Carey as devastated, winded, wounded, and near hysteria. Lucky to be alive and crazed with fear and guilt, Charlie added. As Charlie Miller talked on, Muriel listened to a frightening dialogue between two men caught in a tragedy with tentacles reaching 23 years beyond the past.

****

Charlie: You belong in the hospital, man. I've got the car, let me drive you down to Quayville.

Carey: No, no! We can't leave here! He could be out there, anywhere! Charlie, sorry, so sorry, but I have to tell you – Marchman, he killed your mother. Almalene is dead; I couldn't stop him; I couldn't save her.

Charlie: You saw them! You witnessed it?

Carey: Oh God, it's my fault! I didn't hurt her; I cared for your mother, Charlie. But it's my fault he killed her. We were together and he found us.

Charlie: Try to calm down and breathe. Tell me what happened, from the beginning. He told me he was going looking for her. Where did he find you?

Carey: Across the stone bridge, on the towpath side. We left Ted's inn with a bottle of whiskey but we were already drunk. We stopped on the bridge, you know, above the water, but later we walked into the trees. We were in the clearing there… And that's where he came upon us. I think… Charlie, I'm sorry, I think I'm going to be sick.

Charlie told Muriel he left Carey at the table and took an old pan from the kitchen and put it on top of the table for Carey to use. He also brought a glass of water to Carey, but Carey turned away from both offerings. Charlie also told her that he felt way older than 18 that night, and Carey seemed younger than his 23 years. Charlie worried that Carey might die.

Carey: Thanks, I think I'm okay now. I hurt but I can breathe a little. Pretty sure he broke ribs, but I know I'm lucky I'm alive.

Charlie: For now, anyway. So, you and Almalene were in the clearing when he found you. What happened?

Carey: We had clothes on; it's cold in November, but … I was on top of her. He pulled me off of her and socked me a couple of times and threw me off to the side. I tried to get up but he hit me hard; I couldn't stand up right away and he was on her, strangling her.

Charlie described Carey's struggle to catch his breath to Muriel and told her that he finally drank a little water before he could answer Charlie's next question.

Charlie: He strangled her before you could get to your feet. Then what happened?

Carey: No, no, I did stand up and she was still alive. I started beating him on the back with my fists, and he got off her and hit me in my face and throat and kicked me back down. Then he kicked me while I was down and stomped on my face and went back to her. I was praying she ran away while he attacked me, but she didn't. Maybe she couldn't; she just lay there, like she was frozen to the ground. I can't … I couldn't …

Charlie: Try to relax and breathe, Carey. It's over; it's done. Just tell me the rest, but slowly, calmly. You did your best; you tried. You're safe in here. Just tell me.

Carey: He was strangling her with one hand and hitting her in the face with his other hand, his fist. I screamed and tried to get up but I couldn't. Charlie, she didn't fight back. She just lay there and let him strangle her to death. Then he got up off of her and ran away through the woods. He was screaming, making like a howling sound, and laughing at the same time.

Both Muriel and Charlie were silent for a minute or so, as they took in the chill of horror that Carey must have felt. Then Muriel, and perhaps Charlie also, saw and listened to Carey again.

Carey: I felt like I couldn't get my breath and I might pass out, but I was able to crawl over to Almalene and I tried to revive her. I did, Charlie, I tried, but I was too late to help her. I pulled her dress down and I dragged her out of the woods, down near the towpath so she could see the water. She always told me she loved the water.

Slowly, Carey faded from Muriel's view and she saw and heard only Charlie. He told her that Carey cried twice while he spoke about what happened. Carey had cried when he said Almalene did not fight back and he cried when he said she loved the water.

After a deep sigh, Charlie explained to Muriel that even though he urged Carey to call his father, Carey insisted that no one, not his parents, no one could know the story. Just him and Charlie. If Hal knew and was questioned by the sheriff, he'd have to lie or implicate Carey as a witness or part of the crime. Maybe as the cause of the crime. Carey told Charlie his parents could never know; it would be too hard on them.

Charlie told Muriel that Carey was gasping and intermittently groaning throughout his terrible story and again he begged Charlie not to say anything about this to Hal or Louise Walsh, and not to tell the police or anyone else. Charlie said he promised but advised Carey to let Charlie drive him to the hospital.

Carey refused and asked Charlie if he could stay overnight with Charlie and for a few more days until he recovered somewhat, at least enough to go to work at his construction job in Quayville.

Charlie ran a hand over his face and back through his hair, and gave a slow shake of his head.

"I asked him if he was crazy, how could he go back to work all banged up like he was. Wouldn't his boss ask him what happened? He said he'd make up some lie and they needed workers so badly that as long as he could manage to do what needed done, they'd let him.

"So, I agreed to let him stay and hid him in my secret rooms here on the ground floor, in this apartment Carey and I built years earlier at night when my parents were out drinking. I told Marchman and Almalene and Carey told his folks we were building a dark room for my photography. And there was that, but we also put in the rest. Carey knew how to do all kinds of stuff and what I hadn't learned from Marchman I learned from Carey."

Shaking his head slightly, Charlie said, "That's the best thing she did for me, Almalene. This one guy, a john, who came up here from Quayville to sample something different? Well, he chose her because she was wild and looked it. He had a camera with him to take pictures of quaint little Mossmead. He puts the camera on top of a chest of drawers, against the wall.

"Almalene sees that, takes all her clothes off, and has the nerve to make a deal with him. She says she'll do anything he wants and he doesn't need to spend dollar one. Just give her the camera. Well, it wasn't much, just a simple old camera, so he agrees. She gave that camera to me since she'd noticed I was keen to look at pictures. I was twelve at the time."

For the first time, Charlie's voice faltered and he rubbed his eyes with the heels of both hands. He and Muriel sat in silence for a few moments.

"What happened? Marchman didn't come to the shop, did he?" Muriel asked timidly.

"No, he was gone, ran off and never found. Much later that day, early Saturday evening, police, the sheriff and a deputy, came and told me about Almalene being strangled and they were looking for Marchman. They asked to search the place and I said yeah, sure, but he's not here, I would have heard him come in.

"They searched the shop and the flat above the shop, and asked what was the door behind the counter to, and I told them, 'Storage. Do you want to check?' and opened the door, but they said, no, that was alright. They said they were sorry about my mother and if my father came home, they wanted to talk with him, so be sure to call them. I said I would and they left.

"Almost done. Would you like more tea, Muriel?"

"Yes, please. Thanks, Charlie," Muriel was feeling they could both use a break.

After he brought fresh tea bags and poured hot water, they stayed quiet for a bit while they drank soothing tea. Then Charlie resumed his story.

"Carey sleeps most of Saturday morning, then I get him to take some beef broth and he keeps that down and sleeps again. Kind of like he's afraid to wake up. By then it's late Saturday afternoon and they've found the body. I'm getting this out of order, but then they search the shop and leave.

"You should know that there was no coroner in Mossmead then and still isn't one; they have to get someone in from the County afterwards. Dr. Bailey, Mossmead's one and only physician then and now, examines my mother's body and tells the law that whoever killed her has big hands because it looks like she was strangled with one hand and beaten about the face with the other.

"So, the sheriff and one deputy are off searching for Marchman and the other stupid deputy goes out and brings poor Turner Stanhope in for questioning. When they can't find my father, and Stanhope insists he had nothing to do with it, they call me on the phone and tell me they've arrested someone and are questioning him at the jailhouse.

"Saturday night, I wake Carey up to bolt the apartment door shut and tell him he'll have to let me in when I come back and knock, and I go to the station and tell them they need to let Turner go and arrest Marchman since the last I heard from him, he went looking for Almalene and he was pissed as hell. And I say that my father has enormous hands; I know since he smacked me and my mother around enough times.

"After they let Turner Stanhope go, the three of them searched the towpath, the woods, even up in the mountain foothills. They ended up looking off and on for months but they never found him. From then on, Marchman's been gone – he's in the wind."

"No one knows what happened to him?"

"Correct. For all anybody knows, he's living another life in another state or he died up in the mountains."

Muriel furrowed her brow and said, "And Carey stayed with you until he healed?"

"He stayed with me till he barely looked better and could stand up, just Saturday and Sunday, and then on Monday he went back to work in Quayville and stayed there a while with Dale Brand, a friend of his and Lonnie's. Sunday afternoon Carey had called his folks and told his dad he had a work injury on Friday but he was okay, still able to work and staying in Quayville for a few days. Then he hung up before Hal could ask questions. He told me all that later, next time I saw him.

"Hal called me Tuesday morning and asked if I knew how to reach Carey. He sounded desperate but I told him I had no idea where Carey was. I lied and said I hadn't seen Carey for more than a week. As far as I know, Hal doesn't know the truth to this very day.

"And Muriel, you have to promise not to tell him. Carey's parents knew he was having an affair with Almalene and they hated it. But they had no idea he witnessed her murder. I told you because I know you're fond of Carey, but listen, even Deena doesn't know this. I promised Carey so I have to ask you to never repeat what I told you. Please?"

Softly and reluctantly, Muriel told Charlie she promised not to tell. After she offered to rinse out her tea cup, which Charlie turned down, she asked if she could leave now. Charlie offered to drive her home, but Muriel said she wished to walk home. Charlie escorted her out of the building.

Squinting in sunshine that seemed bright after time spent in Charlie's apartment, Muriel slowly crossed the trestle bridge and turned left onto the sidewalk. She picked up her pace as she walked and let her thoughts race over what she had heard. Although she regretted not asking him at least one question that troubled her, she understood that he may not have answered even if he knew the answer.

Halfway home Muriel started to cry.

****

Alone, with his shop closed early, and again locked into his hidden apartment, Charlie remembered an emotional moment with Carey many years after Almalene's murder.

In the extra bedroom where Charlie photographed erotic stills, he had finished a session taking photo shots of a three-way with Kim on her knees in front of Carey in the middle with young Dale Brand standing behind Carey.

Afterwards, while Kim and Dale waited in Carey's truck, Carey made a self-deprecating remark to Charlie.

"I'm wondering.   Am I getting too old to be photographed this way? What say, Charlie?"

Charlie answered, "I don't care how old you are or which gender or how many you fuck. The only person I wish you never had sex with is Almalene."

Carey winced and looked down but said nothing. Charlie's tone heated with more anger than he generally expressed.

"Do you realize I'm cheating you? I pay Kim, Dale, Nadina, everybody except you, for posing, not that much but I always pay them."

Carey said, "Yeah, I do know that."

"So, you know that I'm punishing you?" Charlie snapped.

With melancholy integrity and the faintest of smiles, Carey looked at Charlie and responded.

"I welcome your punishment, Charlie. I welcome it. Don't *you* know that?"

<u>Chapter 16: Burnings</u>

Back at the boarding house after Charlie's revelation, Muriel took her shoes off out on the porch. She opened the front door as quietly as she could and in her stockinged feet tiptoed up the stairs to her room. Safely inside she sat on her bed and cried into her pillow, releasing her sorrow for Carey, Charlie, Almalene, also for Turner, Hal and Louise Walsh, and even for Marchman Miller.

She knew she had to stop her tears before suppertime since she had to keep her sad knowledge private. Muriel had no appetite but she pulled herself together, cleaned Blinky's cat-sand box, washed up before dinner, and felt vastly relieved that Sunday's suppers were light. Although Nadina, Turner and Trudy ate outside at one of the porch tables, Muriel ate in the dining room with Peggy, Tom, and Reed. As usual Peggy was in a talkative mood and Muriel gratefully listened.

Retiring to her room early Muriel got into her pajamas but not into bed. For over an hour Muriel sat and looked out at her vision of Mossmead Hamlet from the highbacked chair by her window. During daytime sunlight she would be able to make out Ossie and Leroy in their turnout, and small human figures going into the diner, plus cars and people traveling downtown.

On this night at dusk, Muriel's vision swept over the entire village: the edge of the river, the two bridges, one at a time and both at once, everything shaped in blue slowly fading into night.

She saw street lights, house lights, headlights of cars, porch lights shining yellow to white all across town or popping on platinum here and there. Each night, life outside her room bathed itself clean and sparkling, just before Muriel went to bed and the respite that comes in darkness.

And every morning, she awoke to a slowly illuminating sunrise exposing again the soiled details, the hidden edges, the unending questions of a village absolutely within her view but deeply beyond her touch.

There had been a man who worked and lived in a tiny trailer on the property at the horse stable on the outskirts of Tylertown. Muriel had heard him say once, "It doesn't matter." He said this at a time when something horrific was happening, some older or broken-down school horses that had been in his care were sent away to be auctioned for slaughter, possibly so as to recoup the stable owners' financial losses. So tragic and sad. Why would he say it didn't matter? Maybe it did matter to him, matter very much, but there was nothing he could do about it. Maybe he felt trapped.

Trapped. At times throughout her adult life with her parents, she had felt trapped – pinned and preserved like a plucked flower pressed inside a book. Now she was free, in a way. She had her own life, her own room. This was her room, she paid for it. Not a large space to live in, but when she looked out her window … What would it matter that her life was restricted if when she gazed out her window, she was free in her mind?

****

That same Sunday night Charlie sat in his bed fitted into a corner of the back wall and read his book for a little while. Then he turned off the light and lay down on his back, facing up toward the ceiling, and imagined he looked into a starlit sky. Soon the sparkling twilight he pictured exploded into yellow, orange and crimson flames dancing threateningly into the heavens.

His memory had taken him back those 23 years to the Sunday night after his mother's body was found. Since Carey slept in Charlie's bed, Charlie lay down on a cot in the extra room next to the actual dark room. But Charlie couldn't sleep and eventually he heard something large moving around outside the building.

Even back then he suspected what was happening; his father had long threatened to burn out Ted Dubbock's business. Right then Charlie discerned that Marchman was using stored gasoline from one of the two wooden sheds out back to torch Ted's tavern. Quickly but quietly, Charlie hurried out to the shop, first, locking the door to his apartment, then bolting shut the front door to the building before phoning the sheriff in Mossmead and the Quayville fire department.

No matter how worried he felt about Nadina and Kim,

and even Ted, since they all lived above the tavern, Charlie knew he could not open the one and only door to the building. If Marchman got in, Carey and maybe he himself would be dead. With cold determination Charlie unlocked a drawer in the storage room and retrieved the object his father kept there. He brought that out to the shop, sat in the chair behind the counter, and waited.

In less than twenty minutes, Charlie heard Marchman try his key in the front door and knew his father would realize instantly that the bolt was thrown. A loud frantic pounding on the door followed, and Charlie got up and walked from behind the counter and out to just inside the door.

In a howling yell Marchman demanded entry, "Charlie! Open this door right now! I'll break in if you don't!"

"I'd like to see you break in when there are no windows on the ground floor and no way to reach windows above. You fixed that yourself if you remember."

"You had better unbolt his door if you know…"

Marchman's voice was interrupted by the sound of sirens as firetrucks roared down the street toward the tavern next door. Charlie put all the outrage from his brutal and neglected childhood into his dry-ice voice when he answered his father.

"No, I will not open this door for you. Never. You had best be going away, Marchman. The sheriff knows you killed my mother and will know you set that fire. And understand this; if I ever see you again, I will shoot you dead. That's right – I found your gun."

Again, all those years later, Charlie closed his eyes and tried to close his mind to the memory of his father.

What he chose to focus on instead was the relief of discovering how Ted, Nadina and Kim had cheated death, escaping from the burning inn without their belongings but with their lives. Ted had moved out of town soon after. Charlie had set Deena up with a live-in housecleaning job with the Vinterbos's, and eventually with her room and board at Trudy's place. And Kim had moved in with Carey.

With his wages from construction work, Carey Walsh had given Charlie the money to bury Almalene. Carey paid for everything: the plot, the burial workers, the slab marking her grave. The words under her name on her small plain gravestone were inscribed forever into Charlie's memory: a life lived wild.

Chapter 17: The Parting

Despite invigorating early September weather while finishing all his regular evening barn-related chores plus a few extras, and eating an excellent fish supper with his father and Kim in Hal's kitchen, Carey Walsh felt down and lifeless, as though he was in a state of shock. Nevertheless, he thanked his dad for the meal and offered to help with dishes, but luckily Kim insisted on taking care of them since Hal cooked and Carey worked all day.

Smiling his gratitude to her, Carey petted the dogs and unhooked their collars and leashes from nails on the side of a tall kitchen cabinet. Ditsy and Suds went right to him and began wagging their tails.

Hal said, "If you wait a minute, I'll join you."

"Thanks, Dad, but I've got this. I need a night walk to unwind from work and I've been missing these guys' company lately. Be back in a little bit," Carey and canine companions left via the kitchen door to outside.

"Have another cup of coffee. Relax for a change, would ya," Kim spoke up so Hal could hear her voice above the water she ran to rinse dishes.

Responding, "Thanks, I will," Hal took a sip of coffee he'd already poured, then asked her, "He seems despondent. Do you think he's all right?"

Kim turned the water off and hesitated a second.

She said, "Yeah, I think he's okay. He's always tired on Fridays after he works all week."

She knew different, but she wasn't going to admit that to Carey's father. In that moment Kim decided to go out to the sidewalk in front of the plot of grass beside the diner after she finished the dishes. She wanted a smoke before she went upstairs to their apartment and took on Carey when he was in this mood.

Three quarters of an hour later Carey returned with Ditsy and Suds. Releasing them and hanging up their gear, he fed them and walked quietly into the house's living room where Hal was watching television.

Carey stood next to Hal's chair until a commercial came on, then patted his father on the shoulder.

"Good night, Dad. I fed the dogs. If you don't need anything else, I'm going out to the apartment now."

Hal absentmindedly answered, "See you tomorrow morning, Carey," smiled at his son and turned his attention back to the TV.

Out back inside the stable, Carey looked into the slow eating mule's stall and said, "Night, Leroy." Beside Leroy's box stall, the big Percheron heard Carey's voice and put his head out over the lower half of his own stall door.

Hugging the horse's neck and pressing his cheek against that magnificent head, Carey said, "Ossie boy," and held on for a moment.

After letting go of Colossus and seeing that barn cat Yolanda was nowhere in sight so Kim had already taken her inside, plus knowing that rabbit Brady was already in his indoor hutch, Carey trudged upstairs to his home of so many years.

Because of what he had learned at work today, and anticipating how Kimberly Hodges could react to that knowledge, Carey sensed that almost everything in his life might be about to change.

Kim heard him on the stairs and opened the door.

"What in the hell is the matter with you? Who died or what disaster happened at work?"

Carey slid past her into the apartment and closed the door before he headed for their bedroom.

"We need to be sitting down for this news," he sighed.

Sitting on one side of the bed near the end and facing a wooden chair next to the closet, Carey took his shoes but not his socks off and waited for Kim to sit.

"You may actually like this," he said sadly. "Our crew leader, Matt, I've worked with him three times before, he told me he got a good job in Erie and the company okayed him to bring one worker along. Matt told me the job could last a year, maybe longer, and should lead to more work. He said he'd help me find an apartment up there if I wanted the job."

Dumbfounded, Kim stared at him before she could find her voice.

"I'd go along?" she stammered.

Carey's look and voice were sad and distressed, "Kim … I wouldn't go without you."

"We'd move up to Erie?"

"We'd have to. At least temporarily. At least for a year or more. But I'd come back down here on weekends, every weekend to help my dad. He's over eighty, Kim, thank God he has Muriel now. Otherwise, I couldn't do it. I still might not be able…"

But Kim was becoming energized. She sat on the edge of her chair and leaned forward toward Carey.

"Honey, your father's animals are old, most of them. They won't live forever, and he could hire someone, one of Trudy's nieces maybe, to clean his place and he does his own cooking when he feels like it. This is our great chance, baby! It might even be the only chance we'll ever get! Your father is tough – he'll do fine. Probably be happy for you!"

"Mules live a long time, Kim. Leroy could last for years yet. Ossie, too, maybe. Their stalls and turnout have to be cleaned every day, that's heavy work for my dad. On the weekends I can still load up the manure and take it to the Clarks and Tuckers for composting, but there's a lot for him to do every day. Plus, he'd be out our rent money since we'll have to pay rent in Erie. I know he gives us a break and he's got money from my grandfather, but still."

Kim asked quickly, "Will the Erie job pay well? As good as the jobs you've had here?"

Carey reluctantly nodded. "It's a huge project. They're building a gigantic shopping mall up there. And they plan to build a housing development next to it. The pay will be the best I've ever had."

Kim started laughing. "Christ almighty, Carey! You're acting like this is bad news when it's pretty much the dream of my life! And like you said, your father does have money and Muriel helps with the animals. Pretty close to perfect, I'd say."

"You're not hearing everything, Kim."

"Well, I am wondering how we're going to get there. And how we're going to move our furniture up there. Is that what I'm not hearing?"

Carey told her, "We're not taking the furniture. The apartment up there will be furnished. And I'll drive us in my car; I'm leaving the truck for Hal since he'll need it and we won't. Matt told me the apartments his uncle has are really townhouses with yards. We can take

Brady and Yolanda since pets are allowed. But that's not what you're not hearing."

"Carey, what you just told me is there's no downside! Why in hell would we not go?"

"Because we'd be the same people, just in a new place, but with the same problems. And when I said I'd come down here every weekend, I meant that I will drive down from Erie every Friday night after work and when I'm not helping my father, I'll be spending time in Quayville with Lonnie. So, you see, I can't be the man of your dreams and you know it. I can't be faithful to you or anyone else. And that's not going to change, Kim."

Kim raised her voice, "Huh uh, you're the one who's not hearing or seeing everything. We don't know anybody in Erie and they don't know us. And that means that I won't be an ex-hooker or an X-rated model to anyone there. Don't you get it? I can maybe get a job, wait tables, something, anything, and I might be able to have friends who don't know my past. My own friends, Carey."

"Yeah, and that's great for you, Kim. But I'll still be the guy letting you down, not being there when you need me. What if you end up just as aggravated with me as you are here in Mossmead?"

Carey moved forward near the edge of the bed and they stared into each other's eyes. Kim gathered all her resolve before she spoke with intensity.

"Oh no, mister, you are not weaseling out of this. You're not escaping from me or denying yourself by saying you're no good, the way I've always done also. Guess what? I've had a change of heart lately. And what I see now is that whoever else's guy you are, you're my guy as well. In fact, you may be the only guy I'm close to who really understands me. You know how it feels to give over to a man."

Keeping steady eye contact with Carey, Kim resolved to leave the ball in his court, to say nothing until he responded to her. Carey stared at her as though what she had said was completely incomprehensible to him.

For several breathtaking moments neither would speak or move. Then Carey dropped his eyes and looked at Kim's wrist.

"What time is it?" he asked her.

When she said nothing, Carey slowly reached over and gently turned her wrist so he could read the time on her watch. He let go of her wrist but did not look up before speaking.

"Eight twenty-three," he said in his hoarse whisper. "Might not be too late. Why don't you start packing while I call Matt and tell him I'll take the job."

Carey raised his eyes to gage Kim's expression but all he could see was her back as she hurried toward the closet where they kept their suitcases.

<u>Chapter 18: Another Day, Another Story</u>

At ten after six on Monday morning September 8, glancing out her forbidden window from inside the diner, Muriel noticed that a light inside the stable was on but the apartment above the barn and Hal's house were dark. She could make out Ossie and Leroy eating hay in their turnout but no humans or dogs, that she could see, were in there with them. Maybe Carey was cleaning the stalls and Hal was sleeping in. Muriel drank her coffee and got ready to start work.

Midmorning after Kay had poured second coffees for the Silas table, she motioned Muriel aside and confided to her in lowered tones.

"Hal's out there tottering around the mule-and-horse pen. Either he got drunk Sunday night or he's finally feeling his age. I think you might want to snap him up right quick, Sis. You never can tell; maybe he's headed for the last roundup," Kay made a funny face to cue Muriel she was joking. Kind of.

Muriel challenged her, "Carey's probably working today and Hal had to do all the barn cleanup. Since you're such a youngster, you don't realize the toll extra effort takes on someone of age. And by the way, I'm not in the practice of 'snapping anyone up' – methinks that's more your style, Miss Kay."

Kay grinned and retorted, "Scuse my French, dearie, but shit no, young or not, my snapping up days are over. Silas is pissed at me, big time. Remember Mark, son of Silas? Mark who was going to be my way out of Mossmead? Yeah, but his father got spooked, thinking that little old me would whisk his son away to the big city, and convinced the brat to drop real estate and take management classes so he can be high and mighty at the steel plant in Quayville. Imagine me stuck with junior boss in Quayville – not happening. Another bubble busted. And in the meantime, this hideous Vietnam war goes on forever."

"I'm sorry, Kay. For both," said Muriel, thinking 'What a relief, she's not leaving. If only our soldiers could leave Vietnam instead.'

Around twenty after two, close to end of shift for Muriel, she saw Hal Walsh shuffle into the diner and sit down at the table where they had lunched together on Saturday. He did move slowly and stiffly and did seem dejected, and using her experienced perception, Muriel realized he may have been crying earlier.

She grabbed a coffee pot and a menu and hurried to his table to wait on him. Closeup Muriel could see that Hal's eyes were bloodshot as he nodded his thanks for coffee and motioned to her to keep the menu.

"Thanks, don't need it. Just fried eggs and hash browns for me today. Muriel, do you think Trudy V will be here any minute for lunch with you? I'd love to steal you for today but I don't want to leave her bereft of a lunch partner without notice."

"You're in luck; she's treating Natalie and Florence

to dinner at the Riverbank Café today. I'd love to join you. Do you want anything to drink besides coffee, other than water? I'm going to have a Coke with my eggs and potatoes."

"Water's fine, you know my habit. Are you sure you don't mind joining me? I'm not going to be thrilling company, not that I ever am," Hal sounded uncharacteristically fatigued.

Muriel said, "I'm happy you asked. Be back in a few," and hurriedly left his table, placed both orders for the cooks, drew the Cola for her fountain drink, picked up a coffee pot and poured Hal another cup of coffee.

When she returned with their lunches, Hal said briskly, "Let's eat, and talk after."

They did, and despite Hal's obvious misery and Muriel's hidden worry, they both cleaned their plates. Hal was smiling while he watched Muriel eat and waited to speak until she had a drink and looked over at his face.

"I don't know how to tell you this, but here goes. Carey got long-term work in Erie, and this past weekend he and Kim moved out of the apartment. They will be gone at least a year or longer, depending on the job. He told me he's driving back every weekend to help with the critters and the place, but he's staying with Lonnie at night since Kim will stay in Erie and they won't need the apartment. Unless or until the job ends."

"Hal, does that mean you have to clean the barn, turnout and pastures every day? I can help when I'm not working, but not every day."

"I appreciate that, but only the turnout on weekdays when you're free and only if you feel like it. You're helping a lot as it is."

Muriel got a distressed look on her face, "What will happen to Brady rabbit?"

"Carey took him and his indoor hutch along and Kim took Yolanda. Which reminds me, could you go to the animal shelter with me after lunch and help me pick out two cats for the barn?"

"Of course, I'd love to. I'll just need to stop at my room and change into my shirt and jeans, then I'll meet you at your house?"

Hal smiled at her. "How about if I drive my truck over and pick you up? Or better yet, I'll give you a ride over and wait in the truck for you. How's that?"

"Yes, thank you. Is Carey okay? I'm sorry, but I worry about him."

"I know, and so do I. He feels he needs to do this, and maybe he's right; maybe it will help him. Honestly, Muriel, I can't say that he and Kim will stay together after it's just the two of them. He has so much guilt; I don't know how much longer she can handle dealing with him. Or how long she's willing to try."

"What makes him so guilt-ridden?" Muriel wanted Hal's take on this subject.

"Um, more than one reason, I think … I don't even know all the reasons; I doubt that anyone does. You've heard about the murder?"

"Yes, I have. You don't think Carey had anything to do with that, do you?" Muriel was working on a dilemma.

"No, not really, but … Carey was missing the day the body was found. And the night before – when it happened. He has never spoken with me about it except to tell me that he had an accident at work on Friday, and then he stayed the weekend with some friend of his and Lonnie's. But the murder happened Friday night and I'm not sure I believe what he said."

Hal sighed deeply and looked to Muriel, who suggested, "But you know your son well enough to know he couldn't have killed her or killed anyone?"

"I'd like to think that, yes, but do I? He was committing adultery with her, Muriel, that much I do know. The whole town knew. The sheriff, Doc Bailey, Charlie Miller all believe her husband killed her, but was Carey involved? When I ask him, he doesn't answer. So, I can't be sure, no matter what I think or feel," Hal's voice and expression were painful.

Muriel said, "He doesn't deserve the guilt he carries over that, Hal. Carey was innocent; he was not to blame for what happened to Almalene Miller. I'm sure of that; someone who knows for sure told me. And I believe that someone told me the truth. That's all I can say about it, but I do need to tell you that."

"Thank you," whispered Hal, his relief palpable. "I want to believe that and I need to believe it's true."

"It is and you're welcome, but I hope you don't mind if I ask you about something I've heard and do not understand. Why do Silas and gang say, 'If only it had been the mule?' Muriel had been pondering this and was a little tormented by it.

Hal waved his hand as though to bat the question or its importance aside.

"Oh, that's just conjecture about something they know nothing about, not really. They think, possibly rightly so, that Leroy would have refused to go farther and…"

Hal paused and glanced around the diner. Muriel lifted her eyebrows.

"I'm sorry. Come to think of it, I'd rather not talk about this subject here. Why don't we go barn cat shopping tomorrow, and instead I'll take you to dinner at Darnell's this evening. I'll tell you all about the mule question and more about Carey's guilt, plus I have a proposition for you. Pick you up at 5:15?"

Nervously, Muriel nodded yes.

Chapter 19: At the Hotel by the River

The Darnell Hotel, on the small side but very elegant in appearance, had three stories and a mansard roof and was indeed located next to the edge of the Quayville River. Darnell's Restaurant could only be entered from a side portion of the hotel lobby and going upstairs to a mezzanine floor.

Muriel wore her dress since Trudy's description of Darnell's was 'very posh, a little pretentious, but the food and the view are excellent. Peter took me there soon after we were married.'

Timid as they crossed through the hotel lobby, Muriel held Hal's offered arm and kept reminding herself to breathe. Hal was wearing a suit and tie and this made Muriel all the more hesitant and anxious. She felt as though she and Hal were marching into a beautiful den of doom.

Yet at the top of the stairs, entering the mezzanine floor, she drew in a quick breath for an entirely different reason. Shaped like a half-moon, the restaurant contained large windows all the way around the outside, and since its center floor was not wide and the river was, Muriel guessed that diners could see the river from any table in the place.

Hal Walsh had reserved a window table for two, and dimmed lighting inside as outside neared dusk, evoked a romantic mood. Their waiter, in white dress shirt with black vest and trousers, assisted Muriel's seating and handed them fancy menus, then asked if he could bring them something to drink.

"Shall I choose a wine?" Hal asked.

Muriel flushed and answered, "Just water is fine for me, thanks."

Hal nodded. "Same here, with coffee for us after, please," he responded.

"As you wish," said their server before he listed the specials and left their table.

Opening the fancy white menu with gorgeous blue print, Muriel had to suppress a sudden desire to snicker. Remembering Turner's past employment at Darnell's, Muriel wondered how improbable it had been for a man like Mr. Stanhope to be as deferential as what might be required. She also wondered how normally down-to-earth Hal could seem so relaxed in this rarefied atmosphere and what tragic tale would be coming her way. She feared this might be one of the worst nights of her life.

Reading her menu multiplied her dread. Prices were not listed. Muriel lowered her menu, thus conveying her horrified expression to Hal.

"This is my special treat so please you are to not worry about prices. I recommend the smoked trout with baked potato, cooked baby carrots with dill butter, fennel salad, and baked bread, and that is what I'm ordering for myself," Hal told her.

Muriel, who had never tasted fennel and had no idea there was such a thing as dill butter, nodded yes to Hal's choice, and he ordered for them.

As soon as their waiter left the table, Hal informed Muriel, "Don't worry, the fish will be fresh and delicious. Quayville is known for its fishing industry, that and the steel mill, so it's a river town as well as a factory town."

Regardless of Hal's reassurance and uncomfortable as she felt, Muriel knew she needed to stay calm and supportive to her dinner companion.　But her trepidation over what he might say or ask of her was huge.

Hal glanced out the window at the river and said, "This place stirs up memories.　I used to bring Louise, Carey's mother, here every year for her birthday."

Gazing out the window also, fascinated by colors: golden ribbons, wide across the darkening sky and narrow through the water, with highlights of silver and blues in the indigo river, Muriel spoke very softly.

"She must have loved that; it's so beautiful here."

"Yes, it is and she did enjoy coming here.　The canal used to be beautiful, too.　We, Louise, Carey and myself, used to host canal tours every Saturday morning. This was a long, long time ago, starting when

Carey was in his teens," Hal stopped talking as their dinners were served.

After they both tasted and complimented the food, but while they were still eating, Hal resumed speaking.

"Our canal boat was berthed in a boathouse out past the Tucker vegetable farm on a plot of land my father used to own and I kept for decades. A plucky little Morgan horse that had belonged to my grandfather pulled the boat for us originally until eventually we retired him after I bought a mule named Leroy."

"Did you train Leroy how to pull the boat?" Muriel asked.

"Mostly, but it was easy, since he's so smart and since my grandfather trained me. We used to harness him and Carey would lead him on Mossmead town sidewalk and then on the dirt and gravel road I showed you during winter weather over to the boathouse while I drove the truck over. Carey would help me get the boat out in the canal and hitch up Leroy.

"The tourists met us at the boathouse. Louise rode over in the truck with me and got the travelers settled in the boat after she took their money. We didn't charge much; we did it for fun and to keep the tradition. Carey would usually lead Leroy back and forth along the towpath and Louise and I would ride the boat and give 'talks' about the canal and town's history."

Muriel noticed that Hal's eyes took on their happy expression while he spoke and she began to relax.

Hal chuckled before he said, "Mossmead Hamlet used to have a little tourist appeal. Our town council, all two of them, even put out a brochure and we, "Walsh Family Canal Tours" were featured in it. More people began riding the boat so that's when we bought Colossus and a double hitch. Leroy and Ossie went super well as a team but when the weather cooled, boats were less crowded and we split them up."

Hal stopped talking and smiled when he noted how Muriel was savoring her fish.

"The fish is excellent, isn't it? But am I talking too much?" Hal wondered.

"How can you talk too much when I'm the world's slowest eater? The fish is wonderful and you're entertaining me while I eat, so thank you."

"This part of the story is where the 'mule thing' comes in. Carey got more work and spent some of his weekends in Quayville with Lonnie and Louise helped with leading Leroy or Ossie so I could handle the boat and do the talks. Except she had problems with Leroy since he could take advantage of her and she let him. Even though 'Oss' was less experienced and spookier, she preferred to handle him on the path or stay on the boat while I led Leroy.

"Okay, on a Saturday over 20 years ago, Louise was

walking with Ossie on the towpath and I was steering the boat behind them. As we rounded a curve in the canal and towpath, and Oss and Louise had just reached the path on the far side of the stone bridge, Ossie spooked and jumped to the side, nearly pushing Louise into the canal. Almalene Miller's corpse was lying on an incline next to the towpath."

Hal, who had finished his dinner and was sipping his coffee between sentences, saw that Muriel put down her fork and stopped eating.

"Are you all right, Muriel?" Hal asked.

Muriel said she was, but all she could hear for a moment was the sound of Carey's words, told to her by Charlie, about how he dragged Almalene's body out of the trees and down near the towpath so she could see the water. And all Muriel could see was Carey's shoulders shaking as he cried against Ossie's neck.

Holding back her tears, Muriel said to Hal, "Louise was okay, wasn't she?"

"I thought so at the time. She did not fall but she panicked and couldn't calm Ossie or herself down. It was extremely traumatic for her; she saw Almalene and knew she was dead. I had to find a tourist willing and capable to steer the boat while I waded across the canal, backed Ossie up a few steps and led him through turning the boat around.

"Then, while Ossie walked along the towpath going

back in the direction of the boathouse, I carried Louise across the canal to the boat and helped her lie down. After that I went back to Ossie, slowed him down and led him the rest of the way. Naturally, the passengers were upset and we refunded their money. That day was the end of our canal tours.

"Since we couldn't call Carey because we didn't know where he was, and Louise was too shaky to drive, walk or ride, she had to wait in the boathouse until I led Ossie back to the turnout, took his bridle and harness off, and then walked back to drive the truck home. As soon as we got in the house, Louise reclined on the sofa and I called the sheriff's office to report finding the body. That Saturday was a hellish day."

Hal sighed and took a break after accepting a coffee refill and a dessert menu. Muriel, starting her first cup of coffee, could tell that Hal's description of the events surrounding the murder was taking a toll on him. Unlike Charlie Miller, Hal Walsh did not seem partially removed vocally or emotionally, even after 23 years.

Muriel showed her concern by saying, "I am so sorry, Hal. The canal tours sound like something you really loved, but I'm glad you and Ossie and Leroy can still walk the towpath. I hope Louise recovered soon and you heard from Carey?"

"Carey did call on Sunday afternoon and gave me the only explanation he's ever spoken about that weekend, the one I told you about. But Louise was worse the next day instead of better. She was so weak and lethargic on Monday that I made her promise to go to hospital on Tuesday morning if she didn't feel better. She was like a cat, Muriel, hiding her illness, it turned out to be possible that she suffered for months and didn't tell anyone.

"But I didn't know that then. On Tuesday, I called Lonnie and then called Charlie, which I hated doing after what he was going through, trying to find Carey. Finally, I called Carey at work; he always said not to do that unless it was an emergency, but it was. I told him I was taking Louise to the hospital and if he could, please come over when he got off work. He said he would be there as soon as he could."

Hal looked out the window for a moment. While Muriel waited, she became aware that as the sky outside darkened, the lights inside the restaurant brightened a little. Handing her the dessert menu, Hal seemed to force himself to continue.

"During the ride to the hospital in Quayville, Louise never said a word but as we made the turn out to the highway, she reached out and touched my arm very lightly. I glanced over for an instant and saw her smile at me. But that was all. When we got to the hospital, I pulled the truck all the way up to the emergency entrance, stopped and set the emergency brake so I could open the door and help her out. I opened her passenger side door and I saw how pale she was and I knew…

"I yelled for help and two nurses and an orderly got her

inside on a gurney and doctors tried to revive her. But she was gone. Her heart gave out. Louise had trouble with Carey's birth; the doctor told us she shouldn't have any more children and later her tubes were tied. She was never strong and there could have been history of heart disease in her family, but I never knew. And she never complained.

"After they told me they couldn't save her, I stayed in the waiting room until Carey got there, I think it was just under an hour later. I had to tell him it was too late, but they let us say goodbye to her together. I was numb with shock, I think, but Carey sobbed and sobbed.

"He looked so bad, I tried insisting he check in, but he wouldn't hear of it. After Louise passed away, it was like Carey couldn't do enough to help me with everything. He fed and took care of Leroy and Ossie and the dog and barn cat we had then and except for the cat, walked them on the towpath. He checked and mended fences, the barn, the house, and became the major groundskeeper of the property. And all of this while he was working full time and helping me build that apartment above the stables so he could offer Kim a place to stay, with him as I found out later."

Muriel waited a moment, then handed the dessert menu back to Hal and said, "Ice cream?"

To her relief, he laughed, the waiter appeared at their table and Hal ordered ice cream 'for both' with more coffee.

Smiling, Hal sighed and said to Muriel, "The apartment. Now, finally, I get to float my idea and offer to you. This is not necessarily but may become permanent. Muriel, how would you feel about moving into the apartment above the barn, rent free? But wait, or you could move into my house since there is a second bedroom. You would be around the animals all the time; they'd belong to you as well as me. And you'd only have a few steps to walk to work at the diner. Think it over, but could you be tempted at all?"

'Why do redheads still blush after they've gone grey?' thought Muriel, looking down at the table to avoid Hal's eyes for a second. To herself she acknowledged the peace she felt because Hal did not propose marriage.

She answered him carefully, "My time spent on your property and in company of you, your animals and Carey means more to me than I can say. But in all honesty, I cannot imagine taking advantage of your offer and living in Carey's apartment or intruding on Louise's memory in your home. I hope you can forgive me and I can still visit you and your family."

Muriel finally managed to look up in Hal's direction. Although she expected and feared to find disappointment and possibly anger, she saw only wonderment and impossible hope.

Their ice cream dessert dishes and coffee refills arrived and they enjoyed a quiet recess, after which Hal leaned forward, opened his arms and extended his hands, palms up as though imploring her.

"Of course, you can visit. How about visiting more often? Keep your room at Mrs. V's, spend time there but also at my house. On weekends, after you're finished work, instead of my meeting you at the diner, I could cook lunch for you and Carey at my house. Muriel, I love your company. I'll be content with just a little more of it. Please think about it; you don't need to give me an answer now."

Muriel ate ice cream and thought about what Hal was offering and asking. Yes, she enjoyed Hal's company also and she could visit with Carey, maybe on most weekends. And yes, she loved Leroy and Ossie, Ditsy and Suds, and she could visit with barn cats she helped find at the animal shelter.

She thought about what else he offered – her choice and only her choice. Also, the absence of demands. She had always worried about being forgotten, that she mattered to no one outside her parents. Sitting across the table from her was a man, older and strange and troubled, who cared about her happiness, her freedom. Who knew she was enthralled with his son, yet proposed a situation that allowed her time near Carey, as well as with himself.

'True,' she realized, 'continuing her life at the boarding house was the kicker for her.' She loved her room and she loved her view from that room. She treasured her friendship with Trudy, Blinky, Deena, Turner, Reed and even Peggy and Tom. She could not and would not give all that up for anyone else.

And Hal wasn't asking her to.

This time Muriel let her tears come as she impulsively stood up, knocked on the wooden table with both hands, and answered Hal Walsh.

"Yes," she said. "I'll visit more often; I'll eat lunch with you and Carey and help with all the animals. But I'll keep my room at Mrs. V's because it happens to be my home. As often as time allows me, I'll share your home and family, but I'll always go to my own home after."

Hal's smile was huge. He stood, turned and opened his arms to her and she walked around the table and into his arms. As they hugged each other, Muriel laid her cheek against Hal's chest.

The life Muriel Dunphy found was more than what she sought.

<u>Epilog: Remembrance (Spring 1993)</u>

He reached the third-floor landing just ahead of her but she was not ashamed of that; he was slightly younger than she and besides, since she represented the buyers, he was showing the property.

"That *is* a climb," she couldn't resist saying.

"No elevators in these older Victorians unless they've been refurbished, and this one certainly hasn't. Your clients are still looking for 'as is' condition, right? And to live here, and even keep the furniture?"

She assured him as he opened the door to the first room at the top of the stairway.

"Absolutely, they are. They are thrilled with the photos and information you emailed to me. This location in such a quaint little village, and in the vicinity of this price, is exactly what they've been hoping for," she caught up her breath as they entered the room.

"And with this view," she added, stepping close to the window and standing beside him to peer out.

He said, "Nice, isn't it? This was one of her best rooms. Did I mention that all six of her most recent boarders stayed the distance? They boarded with her for life, and she outlived them all except for Reed Mosgrove. He's the young man who hired me for this sale, also her executor as a matter of fact. Mrs. Vinterbos loved this house. I almost wonder if she didn't live as long as she did because she hated to leave her home."

"She passed away less than a year ago, you said? How old was she? Or am I too nosy?"

"From what I've heard, she always said she was at least 20 years younger but Reed told me he thinks she was in her late 80s, maybe her middle 90s when she passed. And sharp as ever, he said.

"Trudy was not the usual smalltown widow with children and grandchildren. She willed money to her sister's family, the Medley family, someone named Severn Sagal, and to Reed himself, and she donated the proceeds from the sale of this house to the Mossmead Animal Shelter. Apparently, she adopted several cats from there and one of them, Blinky, her last cat, lived to be over 20 years old! 'Tough and crazy like Mrs. V,' is how Reed put it. But I'm going on and on and you want to check out the house!"

"And the charming antique furniture," she said.

Opening the drawer to the bedstand cabinet wide for her appraisal, he commented, "Charming, but also functional. This old stuff is made to last."

Carefully sitting on the bed, she said, "Comfy also," then added a quick, "Wait! Open the drawer again, please. There is something tucked into the back corner. I want to see what it is."

He opened the drawer wide again and she slid her hand inside, reaching all the way to the back.

She retrieved something small and dragged it out of the drawer which he left partially open.

"Look at this," she said, unfolding a half-sized sheet of lined paper. "Someone has printed something, a poem maybe, on this. Mind if I read it?"

"I don't mind anything you do since you're representing qualified buyers," was his answer.

She read the words out loud to him.

> *This is the start of my slow time.*
> *Who knows how tough it will be.*
> *I'm starting over and learning in slow time,*
> *Learning in slow time, I'm free.*
>
> *It may be too late in slow time,*
> *Too late to hope for romance.*
> *But still, I find myself searching for someone,*
> *With someone, I may find a chance.*
>
> *My heart is waking in slow time,*
> *I know my chances are few.*
> *And yet I'm dreaming of dancing in slow time,*
> *Dancing in slow time with you.*

"Huh," he said, but not rudely, as though vaguely surprised. He closed the drawer.

"May I keep this?" she asked, waving the paper.

"Sure, it goes with the house," he told her.

She winked at him, folded the paper back up and put it in her purse while she withdrew a cell phone before glancing around the bedroom.

"I like what I see. Do you think I can get reception out on the porch? I want to speak with my clients."

"Try it. If it doesn't work, try the sidewalk in front. Let me know what they say? Let's get this done."

"Right away," she said, sounding excited as she closed her purse, shouldered her delicate looking briefcase and still holding her cell phone, left the room.

He walked back to the window and gazed out at the view while listening to her descending the stairs.

He spoke out loud, "Too bad Mrs. V didn't live a little longer so she'd know about the house being sold as a home for someone."

As an afterthought, he added, "I bet old Trudy would remember who wrote those verses."

ACKNOWLEDGEMENTS

My appreciation goes to the 'usual suspects,' family and friends who inspire my continued writing. Some of them even read my books.

First mention belongs to Patty Bowman, one of my two younger sisters and an outstanding writer herself, who always reads the dribble I write and offers praise, encouragement, suggestions and essential corrections. Plus, she lets me use her fabulous photographs on my book covers! And I feel immensely privileged to get to be the first reader of her wildly imaginative novels.

Many thanks to wonderful friend Joan Klengler, who has written many marvelous books, including three mystery / romance series with each novel of every series a fun read, plus page-turner separate novels and even non-fiction. Joan, Patty, and I are like three musketeers of writing; we support each other and that means everything to me.

Esteemed friend Jill Grisham partially inspired this book since she continues to work even though she could retire, and similarly to Muriel, she lives in a socially diverse situation, both of which I thoroughly admire. She and her mother, darling Dottie Grisham, have been treasured friends to me and my sister Patty. Plus, they seem to like our books!

Much appreciation to friends Diana Leonard and Jerry

Vogler who both read all my novels and novellas and continue to support and encourage my writing. And to generous friends: Mary Catherine Dino, and Paula Rincon, who accept my books and offer their inspiration, gifts, and valuable friendship.

Many thanks to family members, youngest sister Debbie Rowland, and Uncle Jack and Aunt Sarah Bowman, who all make me laugh and give me much-needed assistance to keep going.

In addition, I can't forget to thank those who 'feed' me, present and past: Ingolf and Joan Klengler, Dottie Grisham and Jill Grisham, Barbara Harms and Dale Lee, Paula Rincon, Jerry Vogler, Manny Davis and Michelle Pancake, and Adriene Harris.

Special mention of thanks to Larry Edmonds, Patty's friend who let us know how to watch 'pay-for-movies' on "On Demand."

Most or all of the people acknowledged above share a love of animals, as important to me as reading and writing.

ABOUT THE AUTHOR

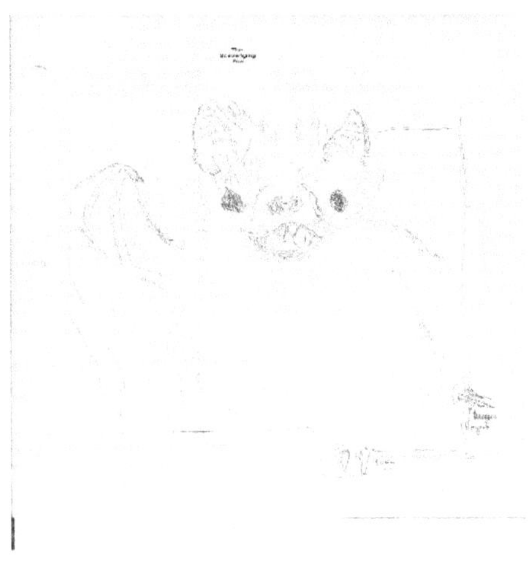

Although born and raised on the East Coast, GRACIE STELLA COOK has lived most of her life in California, many of those years in the greater Los Angeles area with human and critter family members. She worked in the garment, real estate and radio industries, for non-profit conservation and public transportation organizations, and eons ago as a part-time waitress at a bus station adjacent diner improbably called The Terminal Liquor Store.

In addition to DANCING IN SLOW TIME, Gracie has written novels: THE SCAVENGING FEW; IN THE HOURS AFTER MIDNIGHT; STOPPING THE TRAIN; and UNCLE FRANCIS; plus, three novellas: AN EVENING WITH FRANKIE EDGE, THE GOODBYE STATION, and LIKE FIREFLIES.

www.ingramcontent.com/pod-product-compliance
Lightning Source LLC
Chambersburg PA
CBHW071605150726
48000CB00004B/1595